Belle and the edge

Lauren Yule

Contents

Chapter 1 (Belle): Was That Bad?

I'm not sure why Karen always had to be invited to these informal get-togethers, but it annoyed me to no end. She'd walk into Edge's house like she owned it, or at least lived here with him, and then take over as role of hostess, running to get people beers or pop, refreshing the snacks.

The one time I'd tried to help, she waved me away.

"No need," she'd said in a sweet, kind voice that made my fingers itchy with the need to punch her smug face, "guests don't serve themselves here. Edge doesn't like that."

Edge doesn't like that.

What a bitch. With that one statement, she was throwing so many things at me.

She knew what Edge liked and disliked to happen at his home and his gatherings, meaning she'd been there many, many times before.

She'd been with him and acted as his hostess.

She was telling me I was a guest and she was not. Temporary vs. permanent.

Then she'd go serve the other guests because she was letting me know my place and hers. In her mind, I was firmly in the guest category and she was not.

Karen would also stand right beside Edge when everyone was leaving and say goodbye to his friends with him as if they were a couple. As if they were a couple.

She'd actually looked at me from the front door the first night I'd been invited when Edge was distracted with talking to one of his friends and asked, "Do you need to get your purse so you can leave?"

"I'll be here a little longer," I assured her coldly. "But maybe you should go get your purse and get gone."

Her eyes had narrowed on me, but before she could catty back, Edge looked at us.

"Walk me to my car?" she asked Edge. "I'm down the street a ways."

So he'd accompanied her to her car, and -- despite being a guest -- I cleaned up the cups and plates that hadn't made it to the garbage.

Fortunately, Edge was gone less than a minute, and then he made me feel very welcome in his home.

I was standing at the sink when he came back in, washing some wine glasses, and he came in with a few more that he must have picked up when he came back in through the living room. He walked right up behind me and his arms went around me on either side to drop the glasses in the soapy water. Once his hands were free, he curled his arms around my waist, nuzzled my neck and then he pressed himself in close.

Well, hello! Karen who?

"You know I have a dishwasher, right?" his low voice was right in my ear.

"Yes, but I think these wine glasses should be washed by hand."

"Well, I know you have to get home soon and there's better things you could be doing with your hands."

I laughed. "I have some time. I can do both."

"You do both then, and I'll play while you finish up."

His hand moved down my thigh, pulling my dress up with it. "My sweet Belle with her hands all soapy and wet. Are any other parts of you wet, too?"

Could you spontaneously combust from a man whispering low and sexy in your ear?

His fingers hooked into my panties and moved them down, down my legs until they were around my ankles.

"Step out," Edge said, his voice getting that rough quality to it when he was about to do dirty, wonderful things to my body.

I quickly obeyed, knowing from the past that that failure to immediately obey could result in a sharp smack to my ass, and given the glasses in my hand --

"Good girl," he praised my obedience. "Now spread those gorgeous legs of yours, Isabelle. And, sweetheart, keep washing those glasses you insisted washing by hand and didn't want to put in my dishwasher."

Forcing myself to wash the glass I had in my hand, just as I started to rinse it off, Edge's fingers were back between my legs, testing, teasing, sliding through the desire he pulled from me.

"My Belle is so fucking wet, so slick and wet," he crooned in my ear, his voice pitched low. Then he slipped two fingers inside of me, his thumb gliding over my clit, and I gasped at the sudden intrusion. "I was thinking about fucking you all night long, wondering if you were thinking of that, too, wondering if you were wearing those silky little panties I love. I wondered if I should make you sneak off to the bathroom and take them off so I could watch you squirm the rest of the night. Because you're a good girl and good girls don't go without their panties at a party, do they, Belle?"

I gasped at the thought of being bare under my dress at a party with his friends, at the hooded looks he'd shoot me all night, the promises his eyes would be making.

"Don't stop washing those dishes, Belle." His demanding voice startled me back to my hands in the soapy water. "You insisted on washing them, so keep washing."

His voice was thick, but I could hear the amusement. His fingers continued working me, curling inside, hitting that spot before he retreated and tortured me some more.

He bit my shoulder so hard I almost jumped, but I felt the jolt all the way down to my pussy that he was alternately working hard then backing off with featherlight touches, intentionally frustrating me.

"Bend over a little more," he ordered me, and I did, all pretenses of washing the glasses over.

His warmth was suddenly gone from my back, and I felt his breath between my legs.

Oh, shit.

"I could breathe you in all day, beautiful. But I want a taste, too."

His thumbs parted my folds, and he licked me lightly, over and over, teasing me to the point I was ready to beg and plead for more, more, more, and then he moved one hand to my clit as he began seriously working me with his mouth and fingers until I was drenched, until I was about to come on his wicked, beautiful, magical mouth --

He pulled his mouth away and bit my thigh, and I twitched at the bite of pain I had come to realize I loved. "Not tonight, Belle."

What the hell? Edge was denying me my orgasm?

What kind of fuckery was this?

"Hold on to the counter," he directed me.

I did, listening as he stood up and unzipped his pants. I heard the tear of the condom wrapper, and then he was at my entrance, the head of his cock right there but going no further. I could feel him pressing up against me but not enough to penetrate, then pulling away just a bit.

"You wanted to come, right on my tongue so I could taste all of that pleasure you give me," he said in my ear, right before he nipped at my neck. "Didn't you, Belle?"

"Yes," I said, my voice so breathy I didn't sound like me.

He was moving the head of his cock against my slit, moving just enough away when I tried to press back against it to slip him inside me.

"Next time, don't choose the dishes, sweetheart," he said. "I have a dish-washer and I don't get to spend nearly enough time with you, inside of you, beside you, holding you close."

He continued tormenting me until I wasn't even sure I knew my name.

"Should I fuck you now, Belle? My cock is so ready to be inside you, feeling you so tight around me like a motherfucking fist. I want to be deep inside of you, sweet Belle, but maybe you'd rather wash some other dishes?"

By this time, I could only whimper, and he slowly slid one hand up my body until he could wrap his fingers around my throat, tight enough for me to be very aware, but not tight enough to be scary.

"Tell me, Belle, what do you want more? My cock or the dishes clean?"

I used to be able to form words quite easily, but this man riddled my senses. I finally found the one word I needed: "You."

"That's my good girl," he praised me as he slammed into me, his fingers pressing harder against my throat as he filled me. Holy shit, this man filled me, fulfilled me.

And tonight was no different.

The second time I'd encountered Karen, I'd noticed -- like I did the first time I'd met her -- the way she treated Edge as her own in subtle, catty ways only another woman would notice, but this time, her possessiveness was increasing. So after that gathering, as I was getting ready to go home, and Edge was walking me to my car, I'd asked him about her.

"Old friend," he'd said, his voice clipped. It was a tone I hadn't heard often in four months but on the two other occasions I had, it was a clear message he didn't want to discuss something.

"It seems like she's more," I braved.

"Not any more. Don't worry about her."

Men are so good at delivering lines like that. It was right up there with calm down.

Calm down. It's a miracle! Look at that, I'm calm now.

Don't worry about her. Oh, OK, just like magic, she's no longer on my mind!

So I got the message and never brought her up again.

But for the third time, she showed up to his house with his other friends tonight.

And once again, she assumed the role of hostess.

Either Edge didn't notice because...clueless man, or he noticed and didn't care, as long as someone was taking care of shit. But I noticed, and I cared. I kept quiet, though. Edge was sleeping with me, had been for four months, and only in the last month had he invited me to come to these gatherings at his home. He was very close to a number of his fellow Marines and they spent a lot of time together, and I felt like he was letting me into his life a little more, taking steps forward, asking me to meet his friends. I didn't want to rock the boat by engaging in a cat fight.

Yet.

Tonight was the first night the children had come over to his house, too, and although I'd offered to take them home and have my mom come over and watch them, Edge had said they were welcome to stay. He said he'd carry them to the car when the get together ended, then follow me home to help me carry them to bed.

Most likely, he'd spend the night at my place, which is something I had only recently allowed to happen. He was the first man I'd let into my life since my ex had signed away his parental rights six years ago and had taken off for parts unknown. Edge, however, clearly wasn't ready for the three of us to spend the night with him, and maybe he was right. Maybe it was too soon.

In fact, he'd made this a later party so my two would already be conked out in his guest bedroom. But he was the one who'd suggested having dinner together after West's afternoon baseball game and he was the one who had suggested we just put West and Piper upstairs to bed. He knew they went down early and were always asleep by eight, so maybe he figured they wouldn't make an appearance or be a problem.

During tonight's gathering, one of Edge's friends asked for a copy of an article Edge had been talking about, and when he went to his study to print out the file, I decided to run upstairs to check on my children. Quietly opening the door, I saw West, my oldest at eight, pop up in the bed and come running over to me.

"Can't sleep?" I whispered. He shook his head.

"Can I say good night to Edge?" he asked in a soft voice. The two of them had hit it off four weeks ago, maybe because Edge was a hero to my son -- he flies attack helicopters, Mom! -- or maybe it was because he simply liked having a male influence in his life.

I thought maybe we could catch Edge in his study and not intrude on the grownups.

"Sure, but you have to be quiet," I said. "I don't want to wake Piper."

So, hand in hand, we walked down to Edge's study, and then I heard Karen say my name and froze.

"You and Isabelle must be getting serious if she's over here all the time, and now her kids are." Her tone was pure snide with a side order of bitch.

"Lay off," came his curt reply. I could hear his printer spitting out pages.

"Am I hearing wedding bells in your future, complete with an insta-family, Daddy?"

I held my breath, not even realizing I'd squeezed West's little hand tighter.

"Not sure why you keep insisting I'm going to marry her every time I see you, Karen. I have absolutely no plans for a future with Belle. I mean, let's be real -- she's got two kids; she's nothing more than a booty call with baggage."

I froze for a split second, my ears ringing so loud I didn't hear Karen's reply. Spinning around, I quietly hustled West up the stairs and back to the guest room.

"You know what? I'm thinking you'd be able to sleep if you were in your own bed tonight. You want to go home?" I whispered.

My eight-year-old son's eyes held more wisdom than a child's his age should. I had always said, even when he was four and five, that he was a wise child, wise beyond his years. Maybe he was just sensitive, but maybe it was more. Either way, his eyes searched mine for a minute, then he nodded.

I wrote a note for Edge (Took the children home. They weren't sleeping well.) and put it on the guest bed while West slipped on his shoes. Then I had West grab my purse and Piper's shoes while I picked up my daughter and carried her downstairs.

Edge and Karen had rejoined their party and were gone from his study, fortunately, so we walked past that room and out the back door to my car. I snugged Piper into her booster seat, and she mumbled something about cheese before passing out again.

West got into his own booster seat -- he was almost big enough to be out of one -- and I checked his belt before getting into the driver's seat. By some miracle, my car wasn't blocked in and I was able to drive away.

"Mom, what Edge said...was that bad? It was bad, wasn't it?"

Dilemma. I had resolved always to be honest with my children -- except for stories about Santa and other mythical beings that added a touch of magic to their childhood, and even then I'd be honest when they asked for the truth -- but I didn't want to be honest about this. Being honest would hurt my little boy who shouldn't feel bad for anything that resulted from his mother's poor choices.

Wouldn't you know, Edge was the first man I'd fallen for since my ex and he saw me as nothing but a booty call. With baggage. The sheer rage that reference to my children had bubbling up inside me would have to wait.

So I hoped answering West directly would avoid any further questions.

"It wasn't nice, buddy-boy."

"I thought he liked all of us. He came to two of my games."

Divert! Divert!

"Yeah, he said he thought you played really well and that you were a very good batter."

"Then why'd he say mean stuff about us?"

Dammit! Why indeed?

"Well, he was probably just having a grumpy day. You know how you and your sister get sometimes?"

"Yeah," he said quietly.

And that was the last thing he said until we got home. He opened the front door for me as I carried his sister inside and put her to bed. He was already climbing into his bed when I walked into his room.

I pulled the covers over him and sat beside him.

"Mom, are you mad at Edge? You know, for what he said?"

Had he seen the seven calls I'd rejected from Edge?

"Not really," I said lightly so he could tell it didn't matter to me.

That was probably the first lie I ever told my son. With the kind of fury that was coursing through my veins, I wanted to twist off Edge's dick and feed it to him, bite by bite. My children were not baggage, which implied they were burdens. They were not; they were the very beat of my heart and the air in my lungs, and if a man didn't see them in the same light, then that was a man I didn't need in my life.

And, I resolved, a man who wouldn't be in my life going forward. Edge could have left it at me being a booty call. Sure, I definitely would have been unhappy and would have stopped seeing him immediately, but I'd get past it. Eventually. Guys use you and are assholes. But then he crossed the line and brought West and Piper into it. Calling my children baggage? His assholery vaulted me to a completely new level of pissed, past Defcon 1 and straight into the stratosphere.

As I rejected call after call from him, as I left his twenty-seven text messages on Read, I hoped he considered himself lucky that I was just ignoring him.

I had been thinking about how much it might cost to rent a wood chipper.

Chapter 2 (Belle): Ineligible For A Promotion

- -

For two solid weeks, I'd refused to answer the door when Edge knocked. I hadn't blocked his number because I wanted him to know I was receiving his texts...and ignoring them. Same with his calls. His voice mails were all basically singing the same song: What's going on? Why won't you talk to me? Are you and West and Piper OK?

The last one always made me rage. Seriously? Like he cared about my baggage? According to Edge, Suitcase 1 and Suitcase 2 made the girl who was good enough to be a booty call ineligible for a promotion to girlfriend or wife.

Quite honestly, I couldn't figure out why the man was still calling and texting and knocking on my front door after two solid weeks of being ignored by a going-nowhere booty call. For heaven's sake -- Karen was right there, just panting and begging to return to his bed. Why work this hard for a mere booty call? And if he didn't want Karen, he was so gorgeous he'd have no trouble finding a replacement for me, maybe this time finding a woman with no excess baggage. In fact, I was thinking maybe someone should make a dating app for that: Booty Calls Without Baggage.

That night we fled from Edge's place, after West fell asleep in his own bed, I went to my room and buried my face in my pillows and cried. Why was I such an epic screw up when it came to picking men? My children's father just walked away from his two-year-old son and brand new daughter. West had absolutely no memories of him, but I knew the day was coming when West would ask where his dad was and I'd have to try to explain a little bit to him. More could come when he was older. Piper was just a free spirit and I could see waiting longer to tell her.

But after Frank had walked away from us, I had a long talk with myself, and I promised myself since the children had only me, that I would focus on them and on me, no distractions. I needed a plan to figure out how I was going to give my children the best life possible.

First item on the agenda was to get a college education. I was twenty-one years old and I had two children and a high school diploma. That would enable me to work, but I had always wanted to go to college, so I figured why not -- I may as well start now. I didn't need much sleep anyway.

It took me five years to do it, but I did, with a lot of help from a group of other mothers like myself who I found at school -- young, single, with children...oops, sorry, with baggage -- and we formed a group of five. We rented a house together from a very understanding landlady who had once been in our shoes, and it was crowded, but we made it work. We had less rent to pay than if we were each in our own apartments, so that helped with tuition. We coordinated our school and work schedules and made a commitment to stick together until we all earned our degrees.

It was just seven months ago that we all moved into our places, but we were still close and they were still the women I could call on if I needed anything, just like they could call on me.

Once I had my degree, a good job as a web designer and had settled us in our tiny, three-bedroom rental home, I decided it was time for a tiny bit of me time. I hadn't allowed myself to date. School, studying and work took enough of my time away from my children. I refused to add anything that would take away from my time with them.

Four months ago, I'd met Edge through a friend of a friend. We'd all met at a bar one night, my mom had the children for a sleepover and I was feeling happy and free to have a little fun. Edge had introduced himself to me immediately, and it was flattering and an ego-boost I hadn't realized how much I'd needed it. He was charming and funny and intelligent and he listened to me, asked me serious questions about myself. He was amazed I had an eight-year-old and a six-year old, but it hadn't seemed to bother him.

With his friend vouching for him, and my friend vouching for Edge's friend, I'd taken Edge home. And that night, Edge had shown me a lot of fun. For the first time since before my daughter was born, so I was raring to go and it was a long, exhausting and extremely satisfying night.

I'd thought that was it, but he'd kept contacting me. We kept having fun and talking whenever I had a free night. He was exceptionally understanding when I told him my availability was limited because of West and Piper. But we managed the odd dinner here and there and then he began texting me. The texting led to calls at night after the children were in bed. I have to admit, I was beginning to love falling asleep right after his deep voice rumbled a delicious good night, sweet Belle to me.

Then a month ago, he texted late one afternoon to ask me out to dinner (apologizing for the last-minute invitation) and I'd told him I couldn't because I had promised my children a rare night out at their favorite pizza place. We'd found a tiny Italian place that made the best pizza, and the owner and his wife always fussed over West and Piper and treated them like visiting celebrities, even giving them some dough to play with at the table while we waited for our pizza. We loved their Margherita pizza with basil and mozzarella cheese.

Sounds great. Can I invite myself along?

I had to think about that for a minute. This was a whole new level, a whole other layer to our...whatever it was. I'd been thinking so long, Edge had sent a second text.

Sorry if I overstepped, but I'd like to see you and meet them. If you're ready for that.

That text told me several important bits of information. Edge knew how important my children were to me, and he knew that being introduced to them was a huge step. He was the one instigating the meeting, and it wasn't me asking him. So I took that as a positive sign that he was somewhat serious about me.

We'd be happy to have you join us.

And for the rest of that month, until I'd heard him telling Karen we basically meant nothing to him, he'd seen the children at least two times a week, managing to make it to two of West's baseball games and treating us afterward to pizza at our favorite place. He'd also invited us to his place during the day to swim a few times -- and one memorable Saturday, Karen had stopped by while the four of us were splashing in Edge's pool. That had surprised both Edge and me, but he'd gotten out of the pool and, after drying off that mouth-watering body, he'd walked her out and come back to join us in about two minutes, an irritated look on his face. This was after the first two gatherings at his place, so Karen and I had already met and declared a polite war.

So hearing him call me a booty call with baggage that had no future? It hurt. Deeply. But more than the hurt, it infuriated me.

Hearing him call my name as I let the children into the house after picking them up from after-school care? I'm not sure he was ready for what he was about to face, but I apparently had to face him now. With a quick word to the children to go inside and watch TV for a minute, I shut the front door and turned to face Edge.

He had the audacity to look somewhat irritated, I noticed, and then I thought, bring it on.

Chapter 3 (Belle): Feed The Baggage

E dge stepped up onto my porch and came right over to me. Something stopped him from touching me because his hands made a move as if to grasp my upper arms -- and then he checked himself and let his hands drift down to his sides.

"Are you OK? What's been going on?"

"We're fine," I said coldly.

And then just like that, the concern became tinged with irritation.

"So you're fine but for two weeks you couldn't call me or return any of my texts or, I don't know, maybe answer your door when I came over? I've been worried about you and West and Piper."

"Like...worried in the sense that you'd be concerned over some lost luggage?"

His brows furrowed in total confusion. "What?"

"Why are you really here, Edge?"

He looked even more confused at the impatience in my attitude and tone. "I just told you. I was worried about the three of you. I didn't know why you left my house that night -- West and Piper were sleeping when I peeked in at them, so your note made no sense. And then you fucking ghosted me for no reason."

For no reason...

"So that still doesn't explain why you're here two weeks later. I would think you'd have gotten the message when I didn't return your calls, text you back or answer my door when you stopped by."

Edge took a step toward me. "What happened, Belle? Did I do something?"

Did he do something? That was a really good question. Did making an honest comment about how he viewed my children and me -- behind my back to his former booty call, no less -- count as doing something?

"Does it matter why?"

His lips tightened in irritation. "Yeah, it matters. I thought you liked what we had going on."

No, Edge, I loved what we had going on up until the moment I realized you viewed me as a booty call with baggage. I was falling in love with you, you idiot! And I noticed you didn't say anything about you liking what we had going on.

I shrugged at him. "I guess you could say I just realized we weren't going anywhere. Why prolong the inevitable?"

I have absolutely no plans for a future with Belle. I mean, let's be real -- she's got two kids; she's nothing more than a booty call with baggage.

"Belle, please, talk to me. We were with each other for four months, so I don't get why you'd suddenly cut me out of your life, especially after the last month."

Don't pretend like you're the victim here, Edge. You were playing me, and worse -- you were playing my children!

"As much as I'd love to talk right now, I have to go in and feed the baggage."

For a moment, he looked startled. "What are you talking about? The baggage?"

"Yes, West and Piper. You may know them as my baggage."

"Belle --" he started to say, but I kept going, and my temper was on the rise.

"In fact, Disney's doing a movie about us. It's called Booty and the Baggage. I think it'll be a hit."

He looked stricken, remembering what he'd said, realizing that I'd heard it all.

"I heard you that night," I told him icily, "When you went to get your friend the printout, I went upstairs to check on the children and West was up. He wanted to say goodnight to you, and since I thought we could catch you in your study, he and I went down there. But we heard Karen insinuating you were going to marry me. And you said you had no plans for a future with me because I was just a booty call with baggage. You said that, and you said it to Karen and I overheard it and worse, West overheard it."

"Belle," he said.

"So thank you for letting Karen know the status of our relationship before you let me know. That meant a lot to me. But have no fear -- I've been letting my friends know the status of our relationship for the last two weeks, too."

"I didn't --"

"But most of all, thank you for letting me know that you thought of the two most precious people in the world to me as baggage, Edge. And West -- oh, he didn't know what booty call and baggage meant, but he knew it was bad. He liked you, Edge, and he thought you liked him. And when you asked to go to dinner with us that night -- and by the way, you asked to join us; I didn't suggest it -- I thought you knew what a huge step that was because I had told you I never dated after Frank left us, much less introduced a man to my children. You asked to come to West's games, you invited us over to swim. You, Edge, not me."

"Fuck," he said.

"Yeah, I know I was good for a fuck, but I stupidly thought that a man asking to be invited into my life and my children's lives knew what that meant to all of us and that it meant something to him, too."

"Please let me explain," he asked, his eyes pleading.

"There's nothing to explain --"

The front door opening interrupted us. "Mom?" West said, his eyes glancing over to Edge before returning to me. "Are you coming in soon?"

Whoa! The cut direct, as my historical romances referred to it.

"Yeah, sweetie, I'll be inside in just a minute. Please get your homework out and have it ready on the kitchen table. And ask Pipe to do the same, please."

And then, before he stepped back inside and shut the door, my little boy shot Edge the most savage look of loathing I'd ever seen on his little face -- and I'd fed this child mashed peas.

When the door shut, I turned back to Edge.

"So, as you can see, we're all just fine and dandy. Feel free to find another booty call with a clear conscience knowing we are done here. But just a suggestion -- this time find a woman without baggage or at least let her know up front that she's just a booty call with no future. And if you're still too much of a coward to deliver the message yourself, I'm sure Karen would be delighted to do your dirty work so she can have you all to herself again."

As I turned to go, his hand grasped my arm.

"Just wait a damn minute," he demanded. "We need to talk this out."

Honestly floored, I just looked at him. "Why would I waste another minute of my time on you? There's nothing to talk about, and there hasn't been since the moment I heard you call my children baggage. Say anything you want about me, but don't you dare say anything about my children!"

"I'm sorry, Belle," he said. "Don't go in yet. If you can't talk about it now, we'll talk about it later but I want to fix this."

"You can't fix calling my children baggage."

"I can. I will," he promised me, his look so determined I was shocked.

"Nope, you really can't because there's no way to pull those words out of my head. They're firmly rooted in there. You meant them. Don't even try to tell me otherwise."

His eyes narrowed on mine. "I'm not going to lie. Maybe I did think that at the time. I hadn't thought things through, hadn't realized just how deep I was in it with you. But two weeks without you has clarified a lot of things for me --"

"Like I wasn't as psycho possessive of you as Karen?" I asked sweetly.

"No. That I want you and West and Piper in my life. I want to explore what we had."

"Unfortunately, Edge, there's no going back at this point, not now that I know what you think of the three of us and that you chose to share it with Karen."

"Karen is not part of this --"

"She's very much a part of this. She's always been in my face about you, and you chose to tell her I was a no-future booty call with baggage."

"I'm going to make this right, Belle. I'm not going to give you up."

Shaking my head, I just looked at him. "You already did. Now I'm going inside, and as soon as that door closes, I'm never going to think of you again."

And I went inside.

And I shut the door.

But I couldn't keep that third promise, no matter how hard I tried.

Chapter 4 (Edge): Put In My Place

T here are certain moments in your life when you realize how many motherfucking swear words you know.

When Belle shut her front door in my face, I went through them all. Every. Single. One. Well, I'd wondered what the hell had happened when she left my home suddenly that night and then went no contact for two weeks.

Her bullshit note seemed to be a lie, based on West and Piper sleeping soundly when I poked my head into the guest room to make sure they were OK. All of the unreturned calls, the ignored texts, the unanswered knocks on her front door when I knew damn well she was home now made sense.

I'd figured maybe Karen had said something to her, but she'd denied it when I asked her. She'd just smiled and shrugged, telling me single mothers were single for a reason and I'd walked away from her after that comment, pissed as hell. But I didn't realize -- never dreamed -- that Belle had over-heard what I'd said to Karen.

Karen was a habit and had been around for about five years -- for the first three-and-a-half years as a good friend from the base, then for a year as a non-exclusive friend with benefits. From the moment I'd met Belle, Karen was immediately back to friend only. She'd taken it calmly, shrugging and saying we'd run our course as friends with benefits and agreeing it was time to go back to friends only. Karen had told me her only concern was that we'd lose our friendship since Belle was now in the picture, and most women couldn't handle a man having a good female friend. I'd assured her we wouldn't stop being friends; she'd been there for me when my father had died suddenly in a car accident three years ago, so I didn't want to lose her friendship. Her support during the darkest time of my life had meant a great deal to me. She was there to talk with whenever I'd needed to vent or just talk about the memories with.

She'd told me that I should watch for warning signs of jealousy, like Belle asking what Karen was to me, Belle trying to push Karen out of our circle of friends, Belle saying she felt uncomfortable around Karen. I'd made sure to continue inviting Karen to the get togethers at my house even once I began inviting Belle so they could meet each other and get used to one another. Karen did the shit duties during my parties, like grabbing drinks and refilling food bowls, so Belle could just hang with my friends without distraction. It worked out well, I thought, until Belle had asked me what Karen was to me when I walked her to her car one night after a party. I'd told her Karen was an old friend, hoping she'd drop it.

I wasn't going to put up with jealousy from Belle when there was nothing for her to be concerned about with Karen. I had no feelings for her beyond friendship, nothing more even when we had moved our friendship to one with a physical side.

"It seems like she's more," she'd pushed back at me, clearly on a fishing expedition.

"Not anymore," I'd told her shortly. "Don't worry about her."

Fortunately after that, Belle had dropped it and hadn't said another word about Karen or my past relationship with her. To me, there was no need to discuss a past that hadn't meant anything to me.

Looking back, I realized my mistake. I'd kept Karen around, putting Belle in a situation that was both uncomfortable and awkward. I wouldn't have wanted to be around a former lover of Belle's, even if they were just friends. I wouldn't have been comfortable with another man who knew Belle intimately being at her parties. And even worse, I'd hate it with everything in me if she talked to this other man about me -- about things she'd never talked to me about. It would have pissed me off to have overheard something like Belle had overheard.

After I realized I was still standing on Belle's porch, I turned and walked away, my mind sorting through ideas and plans.

Phase one began two days later. I knew West's baseball schedule, so I went to the complex where he played and looked around for the field with his team's colors. When I found them, I walked over to where the players were still milling around the bleachers, waiting for the coach to call them together for warm ups. I looked over at the concession stand not too far away and spied Belle and Piper standing in line.

West saw me and hustled over, his face angry.

"You can go." This was worlds apart from how he'd always greeted me before, like a happy puppy. He'd never once been rude, but things had changed drastically.

"I'd like to watch you play, West," I responded calmly.

Those eyes, so like his mom's, stared me down. "Go away. You made my mom cry. We don't want you here."

"West, I wanted to apologize --"

"We're not suitcases. Me and Piper, I mean. We're kids."

I wasn't going to insult him by pretending not to know what he was talking about. "I know you're not, West. I was wrong to say that, and I'm very sorry."

Before he could answer, I heard...happiness. Sheer, undiluted happiness that was like a punch in the gut.

"Eeeeeeeeedge!" Piper's sweet-as-hell voice was calling my name, and I looked to the left to see the little blonde pixie running toward me, pony tail bouncing. I looked a little past her and saw Belle stutter-step before regaining her composure and moving toward us, blank faced, neither happy nor unhappy, which was a huge clue in itself. Every emotion Belle felt always played out on her face.

"No, Pipe," West said to his little sister, a tone in his voice that stopped her in her tracks as she looked to the brother she adored. "Remember? He's not nice."

She turned to stare at me after her brother's cautionary words, her big brown eyes looking at me accusingly.

"West said we don't like you anymore," she said softly to me.

And I knew what weight West's words carried with his sister. "I'm sorry to hear that because I still like all of you."

Belle walked up behind her daughter and placed her hands protectively on Piper's shoulders. "Piper, say goodbye to Edge. He has to get going."

The look in her eyes told me if I tried to object, she'd fuck me up.

I shot a look at West who was watching the three of us closely. "Good luck in your game, West. Remember to choke up on the bat."

He moved the bat to his shoulder and slid his hands as far down as they could go on the handle, all the way down to the knob.

Fuck you, Edge. The message was beyond clear. I'd just been put in my place by an eight-year-old boy.

I turned back to Belle and Piper. Belle was looking slightly away from me, while Piper was looking right at me, a sad look on that little face. West walked over to stand right by them.

"Bye, girls, West," I said quietly, and everything in me wanted to stay, especially when I saw Piper's little lip start to quiver, her precursor to crying. I'd seen her cry on two previous occasions and had been done in by her tears and her little sniffles as her mom worked to staunch her misery. I'd been ready to promise to buy Piper anything she wanted if she'd just stop crying. How did any parent handle their child crying? It was the saddest fucking thing in the world.

Belle handled it like a pro, though, and talked calmly and soothingly to her daughter until she coaxed a smile out of Piper and the crisis was averted.

I walked off, trying not to be too discouraged. I'd known there was a great deal of hurt to overcome -- hurt that I'd carelessly inflicted with my words and without thought. I'd known it wouldn't be easy. I'd known forgiveness wouldn't be instantaneous.

What I hadn't known was just how bad it would hurt.

Chapter 5 (Edge): Speak Of The Devil

F or the rest of the day, I hung out in my backyard, kicked back on one of the deck chairs and doing nothing but contemplating my problems. After being shot down by Belle and her children, I felt about two feet tall.

And I wasn't used to feeling like that with those three. Belle had always been starry-eyed happy when she was around me. When I'd met her children for the first time at the pizza place, they'd been so curious and sweet, each vying for my attention from across the table so I felt like I was at a ping-pong match, looking left, right, left, right as they fired questions and comments at me so fast I could barely keep up.

"Did you ever play baseball?"

"Look at the unicorn I drew!"

"What position did you play?"

"Do you want to color with me?"

"I'm pretty fast. Can you run fast?"

"Mommy said for my birthday I might get pink tennis shoes!"

"Do you like playing catch?"

"I like sparkly nail polish. See?"

Belle had let this go on for a bit, an indulgent smile on her gorgeous lips, until she asked them to take a breath. That was the first time, but not the last, that I'd heard her say that to her children. West and Piper knew what that meant, and they literally stopped what they were doing and breathed deeply for a few moments. After that, the questions still came at me, but from one at a time. West would ask for a few minutes, then Piper would have a turn. And through it all, Belle's eyes were shining with pride and love for her children. They were polite and respectful, and although I had zero experience with children, I'd liked them and their funny ways.

So hearing that they didn't like me anymore because I wasn't nice cut me open in a way I wasn't expecting. I hadn't expected to like her children so much; when I'd asked to join her and the children for dinner that first night, it was because I'd missed seeing Belle. I hadn't seen her in five days, and I needed a Belle fix. So when she'd told me she was taking the children out for pizza, I hadn't thought about anything but seeing her.

Sounds great. Can I invite myself along?

She hadn't responded right away. After four minutes, I didn't even see the three dots indicating she was about to text back. So I sent another text, trying to reassure her that having pizza together was up to her.

Sorry if I overstepped, but I'd like to see you and meet them. If you're ready for that.

That time, after only a minute or so, I'd gotten a response.

We'd be happy to have you join us.

And that had started a month of being able to see Belle more often, sometimes with the children, sometimes without, until the night I'd suggested the children sleep in my guest bedroom so Belle could be at the get-together I was having with my friends.

Including Karen.

How stupid could one man be?

Do you want the short answer or the long?

I'd known I was playing a dangerous game with Belle. Right from the first night, I'd known she had two children, but she hadn't talked much about them other than to mention them in passing, thinking we'd be nothing more than a one-night stand. When we'd hooked up again, and then again, she told me a bit more about them, most notably that she'd never dated, not even once, after her husband left her. It was only now that she was done with school and had a solid job that she was going to start dating again.

So we'd...what? Hooked up for three months? It was more than a series of hookups, though. We'd had sex when we could find the time, but we always met for dinner first and we'd begun talking more and more. Then we'd added texting, and then finally I'd added the call before bed. Something in me had liked knowing my voice was the last thing she heard before she fell asleep.

But in my mind, I'd still kept that distance, even once I'd met her children and had quickly become a small presence in their lives. It wasn't that serious. I wasn't ready to be a father, to have an instant family. I was thirty-two and the thought of being responsible for an eight-year-old and a six-year-old was daunting. West and Piper didn't have a father figure in their life at all, so I would be their de facto father, nothing step about it. Too much responsibility, my mind had whispered. So my mind kept it light, easy. Definitely not serious.

And when I'd said what I said to Karen, I'd even meant it.

At the time.

But why had I said it out loud, even if I'd felt that way? Why had I said it to Karen, who had been giving Belle shit that I didn't even know about? Because Karen had been poking and jabbing at an open wound -- my fear that Belle would want to get married and make me a daddy to her two children. So then I blurted out my booty call/baggage comment, never dreaming both Belle and West would overhear me saying there was no future for us.

When Belle removed herself so completely and thoroughly from my life, I realized pretty damn quick that my heart hadn't gotten the memo on what spewed out of my mouth.

I'd missed her, missed my Belle in such a way that I was surprised.

I'd missed West and Piper, too. Only a month in with them, and I'd missed them and their big little personalities.

Why does shit -- hurtful shit -- come out of our mouths so easily? Why isn't there a giant hand ready to slap itself over our mouths before we destroy a good thing that we didn't know was a good thing because we'd been treating it so casually?

And now I wasn't nice and West and Piper didn't like me any more because I made their mother cry and called them suitcases.

We're kids.

Right now, West was more of a man at eight than I was at thirty-two.

And stupid man that I was, I'd played right into Karen's hands. She'd warned me about things happening with Belle that any normal woman would ask, but Karen had planted the seed in my mind that if Belle started to ask certain things, that meant I was dealing with some jealous woman who would try to end our friendship.

Speak of the devil, I thought as my phone buzzed. Karen had been calling me relentlessly since I'd walked away from her the day she said single mothers were single for a reason. I hadn't texted her or called her, even though prior to our fallout we had talked to each other several times a week and texted daily.

I needed to talk to Karen, explain to her that I was going to pursue Belle, and Karen and I would need to stop the calling and texting. Based on the little Belle had told me on her front porch, I needed to make it clear to Karen that our friendship was a thing of the past. If she pushed, I'd simply tell Karen that her treatment of Belle had made the break necessary.

"Hey, Karen," I said, my voice neutral.

"Finally!" she said and her displeasure was evident. "I've been feeling a little ghosted, Edge."

Wanting to cut right to the chase, and not wanting her over at my house for this discussion, we agreed to meet at an ice cream and coffee shop not far from my house.

When I walked up, Karen was already outside waiting for me, a bright smile on her face.

"I'm hungry since I haven't had lunch," she said. "Can we eat at the Sandwich Shop next door?"

I shrugged, not really giving a damn, just wanting this over with.

We walked into the restaurant together and followed the hostess to a booth. Karen suddenly slipped her hand into mine and gripped mine so tightly I needed to pry her fingers away. But before I could shake her off, she was stopping at the booth closest to us.

"Hi, Belle," Karen cooed. "Having a good date?"

Belle. Having a cozy lunch with West's baseball coach.

Chapter 6 (Edge): Assistant Coach

Belle looked up at Karen and me, startled, and then irritation quickly spread over her features. As soon as I'd seen Belle, I realized why Karen had grabbed my hand right before we reached the table, so I shook my hand once to dislodge her grasping claws.

"Well, nice to see you," Karen said to Belle, "and we'd love to stay and chat, but Edge and I are here for a lunch date and --"

"We're not here for any kind of date," I snapped at her, her eyes widening at my tone. "We were meeting for coffee so I could explain to you why we could no longer be friends since I plan on pursuing Belle and you're an impediment to that with the way you treated her."

Karen's mouth dropped open but she was too surprised to say anything.

"You dragged me over here because...what? You saw Belle walk in here? You saw another chance to be a bitch to her?"

She snapped her mouth shut, then opened it again to say something.

"Not interested in anything you have to say. Get gone."

Karen's face turned red, with embarrassment or anger I wasn't sure and I didn't care.

"You're still here," I said ten seconds later, pissed I'd let myself put up with shit for too long. She wasn't to blame for me losing Belle -- that was completely on me -- but the bullshit that she'd pulled with Belle that I'd been fucking oblivious to hadn't helped, nor was the fact that we'd once been friends with benefits. Karen couldn't be in my life in any way if I were to have any hope of getting Belle to forgive me. It wasn't even a contest between the two women.

Glancing from me to Belle and back to me, Karen lifted her chin and brushed past me, knocking my arm with her shoulder as she left.

Now to deal with the bigger problem. The fact that Belle was having lunch with West's baseball coach was burning in my gut. Apparently, she hadn't wasted any time moving on from me, which was going to really fuck with my plan of getting her back.

I stuck my hand out to West's coach. "Edge Camden."

He looked at Belle and then back at me before shaking my hand. While remaining seated, no less. "Rob York."

Lame handshake, I thought.

I turned my attention back to Belle. "Could I have a quick word with you, please?"

Belle started to open her mouth, but Rob beat her to the punch. "I need to run to the bathroom, so feel free. I'll be right back."

He walked off, and I could see that him leaving -- more specifically, him leaving her here with me -- didn't sit well with Belle. I quickly slid into the seat Rob had just vacated.

Belle leaned toward me across the table. "You have a lot of freaking nerve, you asshole!"

I held my hands up. "I just wanted to talk with you for a minute. I had no idea I'd see you today, but --"

"Yeah, I'm sure you didn't, what with your date with Karen and all."

"It wasn't a date. I swear to you that I was only meeting with her to tell her that we couldn't be friends any longer because I was going to get you back."

With a laugh, Belle sat back in the booth. "You may as well keep her as a friend, then, because you and I are not happening. I've already seen how that movie ends and let me tell you, it left a lot to be desired."

"Belle, listen to me. I need to explain things to you. I want you to give me a chance, to just talk it out with me. We were good, Belle --"

"I thought we were good, Edge, but found out just how wrong I was. Fortunately, before we got any deeper, I found out what you thought not only of me, but of my children as well."

"I don't feel that way --"

"Suddenly, miraculously, you've had a change of heart about my baggage? Why don't I believe that?"

"Belle, c'mon, I made a mistake in saying that. I shouldn't have said it."

"You shouldn't have said it is right, but you meant it, Edge. You didn't want to be an insta-daddy to my children, did you? Maybe if they were a little younger? Maybe if there was just one?"

"Belle, I didn't even know if I wanted children. I was feeling the pressure and I said the wrong thing."

That stopped whatever she'd been about to say.

"You didn't even know if you wanted children?" she demanded. "And yet you asked to meet my children? You, Edge. You asked to meet them and you asked to start doing things with them. Not me. You. So why the big push, then? Why meet them and attend games and have dinners and let us into your life?"

"Because I liked them," I said. "My head may not have been sure about children but that doesn't mean I didn't like them."

"No, Edge, you didn't like them if you could talk about them the way you did. You said yourself you saw them as baggage, and that there was no future for the booty-call and her baggage with you."

"Can we please forget that?" I asked. "Just chalk it up to my overwhelming stupidity and realize I don't really think that way?"

"Actually, I'm really grateful you said that. I'd never thought of myself as a booty-call kind of girl before, but when I set up my dating profile, I advertised myself as a girl with some baggage looking to be a no-future booty call. Well, Edge, I can't even tell you what a fab-u-lous response I got to that! I put up my profile late one night after the baggage were in bed, and when I woke up the next day, I had twenty-six guys who wanted to hook up, no strings attached! And all because of you changing the way I looked at myself! Now, my calendar is full...and so is the old booty, if you know what I mean. And hoo-boy, some of these guys are freaks in the sheets and I'm learning all sorts of fun things. Really expanding my booty-call repertoire, if you will, but since it's just a bunch of one-night stand, no-future hookups, who the hell cares?"

By the end of her rant, her eyes were blazing, and I thought if she realized just how close her fork was to her hand, she'd probably stab me with it. Multiple times.

But Rob returned before I could say anything, looking between us in confusion, wondering about the clearly pissed off look on Belle's face.

"You OK, Belle?" he asked uncertainly. "We can set up the parent roster later and go over what you need to do as the parent coordinator. It doesn't have to be now."

"No, my mother has the children, so I'd like to get this taken care of today," she said, trying not to sound like she wanted to kill people. Me. "Edge was just leaving, anyway."

Taking my cue, I got out of the booth, held my hand out to Rob and we shook hands again. The thought occurred to me that since this wasn't a date, that meant they had driven here separately.

Perfect.

From my vantage point across the street in a bakery, I watched Belle and Rob leave the Sandwich Shop forty-five minutes later, Belle carrying a clipboard I hadn't noticed before. She took off to the left and Rob went to the right. I hustled across the street, following Rob, catching him just when he reached his car.

He looked up at me as if I was about to beat the shit out of him.

"Hey, no, it's all good," I said, holding up my hands to show I was harmless. "But I've been doing some thinking..."

And that is how I became the assistant coach of West's baseball team.

First practice was in two days, and I started making my plans.

Step one in winning back my girl and her children.

Chapter 7 (Belle): Audacity

S ince it was my turn to bring snacks and drinks to practice, I was lagging behind West and Piper as I rolled the cooler behind me. West was carrying his helmet, bat and glove, and Piper was carrying the bag of granola bars for me. Making our way to the bleachers, we settled there, West running ahead to the team's dugout.

I was chatting with a couple of the other moms, one of them, Monica, a single mom like myself, and Piper was chattering animatedly with her group of girls.

"Welllll, hel-lo, handsome," Monica suddenly interrupted our discussion of the snack schedule. She nodded at me. "Your man sure fills out a pair of jeans very nicely."

My man? -- Oh, no. Nope, nope, nope. I turned and saw Edge walking toward the ball field. He looked right at me, smiled, then held up his hand to wave hello, but continued walking toward the coach who greeted him with a huge smile and a handshake. They talked a minute, then Coach handed Edge a clipboard and a Slayers ballcap that Edge immediately fitted onto his head. The two men continued talking for a few more minutes, and my eyes bounced from them to West, who was eyeballing Edge, a little storm cloud building on his face. My boy's eyes shot to me and I shrugged, as if to say I didn't know why Edge was here, talking to Coach.

Before West could come ask me what was going on, Coach called the boys together and we all listened as he explained that Coach Edge would be helping out the team and would be third-base coach during the games. During practices, he'd help with fielding and batting so Coach could concentrate on the three pitching and catching teams and strategizing plays.

West threw me a grumpy look that broke my my heart...and somehow also managed to accuse me at the same time. If Edge and I had been together, my little boy would have been over the moon that Edge was helping to coach his team. Now? My son looked ready to take a bat to Edge's knees. I might even help him.

Coach ran practice a little differently since he now had some official help (Guys, Coach Edge here played baseball for a D1 college team!). He took the six pitchers and catchers on one side of the field and sent the rest of the team over to Edge on the other side of the field.

Edge began working with the boys on fielding techniques, helping them practice by hitting ground balls and pop ups to them, then having the person who caught the ball in the field throw it to the player standing next to Edge, who would toss the ball to their new coach. Then the boy who caught the ball would run out and replace the boy who threw the ball, who would then run to the back of the line.

The drill was going fine until it was West's turn in the field. He dropped the pop up, then frustrated or a little embarrassed or maybe just plain pissed off, he threw the ball as hard as he could right at Edge. I gasped as the ball headed straight for Edge's face. At the last second, he popped his hand up, right in front of his face, and caught the baseball barehanded. We all cringed at the loud smack we could hear from the bleachers as the ball hit his palm.

Edge marched right to West, and I had to resist running out there. To protect my boy? I should have known better. Mad as I was at Edge, he'd been nothing but patient and fair with my children. He crouched in front of West, speaking quietly to him. West looked away from him, and after what seemed like a long time, he looked back at Edge and I saw his little mouth moving.

Edge gave him a nod, stood back up and resumed practice while my boy ran the bases three times before resuming his place in the fielding practice line.

His face was a bit sweaty but I didn't think he'd be throwing a ball at his new coach's face again. I knew I would have to discipline him later....but I was sorely tempted to lecture him while he ate a hot fudge sundae that I wanted to make for him. Not as a reward. Pfft. No. That would be terrible parenting. It would simply be for the purpose of restoring his sugar levels after practice.

Monica sidled up to me when West was running bases. "Someone got in trouble," she said. "But that would have been a real crime if the ball had damaged his face. You hooked yourself an honest-to-goodness hottie. Although, you've missed a chance to play naughty nurse to him tonight."

My mouth tightened, not wanting to tell the team gossip that Edge and I were no longer an item, but also not wanting her to think we were still together.

"Edge and I..." What? Broke up? That would mean we'd actually been something but he'd made it clear in his comment to Karen that were were nothing but a hook up. Stopped fucking just didn't seem like the right way to end the sentence at a Little League practice. So I settled on the option that seemed safest.

"Edge and I aren't seeing each other anymore."

Monica's eyebrows shot up, and then a wicked smile stretched her lips. "Oh, you poor, delusional girl. He isn't here coaching for the sheer love of the game."

At that moment, Coach called for a break before the boys would continue practice by playing a couple of innings against each other. Monica's head snapped over to the team, then back to me.

"Watch and learn something, Belle. Maybe open your eyes?"

With that cryptic statement, she sauntered over to Coach and Edge, who were looking intently at something on the clipboard. She began chatting with them, and then subtly shifted her body until she was facing Edge and Coach was at her back. Coach shot Edge a grin, then walked away, leaving Monica alone with the new coach.

Monica arched her back, thrusting the perfect breasts her ex-husband paid for right into Edge's line of sight. She fluttered a hand to her chest, just in case he'd missed the thrusting, then moved that same hand to his bicep.

Barf.

Whatever.

She's welcome to him.

But surprisingly, Edge immediately stepped back out of her reach, said a couple of words...and walked away.

Grinning all the way back to me, Monica stopped just outside of my personal space bubble and flicked her hand over her tall, shapely body.

"Objectively, Belle, I'm hot as fuck. That's not me being conceited, that's just a fact. My face, my body, my sparkling personality -- I'm the whole package. Men notice me, men want me and I never have to work for them. Ever. I just did the equivalent of a full court press on that man and he didn't even notice. In fact, he backed away from me and went straight to the boys. So either he really loves Little League baseball and just happened to volunteer for your son's team...or that man is making a statement and his statement is I'm coming for you, Belle."

There was so much in what she just said to me that I didn't even know where to start addressing things. But I didn't need to because she just kept going like a runaway train.

"My guess is he massively fucked up with you somehow. My next guess is he's about to start fixing what he broke in a big way."

"I honestly don't know why he's coaching," I told her, "but I can guarantee you that it's not for me. He made his feelings about me very clear."

"You just keep your head buried in the sand," she said, laughing softly. "It's adorable. I'm just going to sit back and watch the fun."

A few minutes later, our attention was diverted when the boys split into two teams and began a game. We watched them play for the next half hour before Coach called it a night.

The boys came running over to me to grab their water bottles or juice boxes and Piper, my little helper, handed out granola bars to the players. Once all the boys had scattered to their parents, I was closing up the cooler when I saw Edge walk up beside me. West and Piper were still talking to friends, so they hadn't seen him close in.

"Hey, Belle," he said. "You look beautiful."

"Sorry about the incident with West," I managed to say while ignoring the compliment.

"I talked to him and he apologized."

"That's good," I said, still feeling lame and unsure of myself, Monica's words ringing in my ears.

"I just wanted to make sure you're OK with me helping to coach West's team."

I shrugged. "Seems to me like the time to ask about that would be prior to becoming the assistant coach. But it doesn't matter. It's a done deal now so no use fighting it."

"I'd like you to stop fighting a lot of things, Belle." He took a step closer to me. "Deep down, I know you'd like to stop fighting things, too."

I shot him a nasty look. "You have no idea --"

"I do, though. I know what I said cut you deep. And I'm sorry for saying it and for hurting you, but I'm not giving up, Belle. I want your forgiveness and I want you back in my life."

"You need to give up on me and focus on some other woman who suits you better. Unfortunately for you, all the single mothers on the team won't make the cut since they all have at least one piece of baggage."

"Just letting you know what to expect," he had the arrogance to say, completely ignoring my baggage comment. "I'll give you time to get used to it, but we're happening, Belle. Fight it all you want, but I'll win you back in the end."

He leaned closer. "You won't be able to help yourself."

Then Edge walked away before I could even find the words to tell him just what I thought of his audacity.

Chapter 8 (Edge): Uncle

When you're trying to win back your girl, if there were rules for this sort of thing, the first rule would probably be Don't make her any more pissed off than she already is.

It's basic, common sense. Any idiot could figure that out.

I was not an idiot. Well, normally I wasn't an idiot.

So how did I fuck up so badly that she was now angrier than ever at me and I was standing on her porch, about to knock on her door, determined to get her to accept my apology -- although my presence could possibly piss her off even more than she already was.

I was staring down the pitcher and had two strikes under my belt. I could not afford a third one.

For a man who always had a plan, I was at a loss here. How do you make someone listen to you and forgive you when they'd just as soon have your head on a platter?

Since I became the assistant coach two weeks ago, I'd been frustrated with the lack of progress with Belle and West. Piper, when no one was looking, would look at me shyly and wiggle her fingers at me in a little wave. I always smiled when she did that and waved back, then she'd duck her head and look around to make sure West or her mom hadn't seen her greeting the enemy. That killed me a bit that she felt she had to do that, and I chalked up another fuck up on the scoreboard.

But I wasn't backing down. No matter how long it took, Belle was going to see that I meant business. I regretted my words and hated that I hurt her and she was going to realize that we belonged together. She was also going to know just how aware I was that she was a package deal -- and the children were bonuses, not baggage.

Every practice, I'd stroll up to Belle to say hello during the break, hoping there'd be some softening in her face, her body, her attitude.

Spoiler alert: there wasn't.

I didn't let that stop me, and I think some of the team mothers actually enjoyed watching me strike out every single practice and after every single game. I felt their eyes on me and they all just melted away as I came over to Belle. She was what I called coldly polite to me; she'd answer my questions with one-word answers and not ask me anything back. Her hands would begin to fidget, a sure tell of hers that she was agitated, and I'd end each conversation the same way, my voice low so the other moms who were eyeing us couldn't overhear: "I'm not giving up on you, on us, on all of us, Belle."

Then, before she could come back at me about what I'd said, I'd tell her to have a good day and I'd walk back over to the dugout.

Her son wasn't any more open than his mother, either. West was just this side of respectful, having somehow learned how to walk the line between I will be polite and I want to kill you. I could tell he despised when I gave him advice, the same as I did with the other boys, and he accepted my suggestions, but I could see in his eyes that he did not want to use any of the techniques and strategies I offered.

But the boys were on a winning streak, so they all -- even West -- listened and learned.

For two weeks, I was continuously running into a brick wall, the only hopeful sign being those brief finger waves from Piper. Otherwise, I was still being shut out and shut out hard.

And then, today, I completely blew it. Like blew it so epically that even I wasn't sure I could come back from this.

On Saturdays -- game days -- I always arrived at the baseball field half an hour before the boys were due to arrive. I set out what equipment I could and double-checked the roster of who was playing which innings. When the boys started trickling in, I checked them off the list, had them pull their bats and gloves out of their bags, and begin warming up by playing catch with their teammates.

As always, I had one eye on the boys and one eye out for Belle and her children. My eyes immediately spotted her as they began walking in from the parking lot.

Hold the fuck on.

This was new and entirely unwelcome twist, not to mention an unexpected one.

Belle was walking toward the field next to a man who was holding Piper's hand. West was walking backward in front of the man, holding his baseball bag, and I could tell he was chattering animatedly at the man because his free hand was waving to emphasize whatever he was saying.

All of this was happening under Belle's watchful eyes, a sweet, indulgent smile on those plush lips. Lips that were smiling at a man who was not me.

My mood suddenly soured.

Then I heard West yell to the man, "Watch me warm up, Uncle Landry!"

And my mood shot straight to hell.

Uncle? Seriously? I was downright snarly now, and only Rob blowing the whistle to call the boys to huddle up so they could practice for fifteen minutes before the game stopped me from heading over to Belle and Uncle Landry and asking what the fuck was going on.

Somehow, I managed to watch the boys as they warmed up, calling out specific pointers to various boys. I almost made West run four laps around the bases for no other reason than he smiled at Uncle Landry and gave him a little wave.

Don't get too attached, I thought. Uncle Landry's going away real soon. I'd be damned if this pretentious prick was going to take my place. This idiot was no good for her, and if she couldn't see that, I'd be pointing it out to her. Right after the game.

Somehow I made it through practice, made it through all the endless innings of the game, my attention often diverted from the game as I watched Piper fawn all over the asshole, who was sitting next to Belle.

He was sitting next to my Belle, and I wondered if my aim was good enough to hit him in the head with a baseball. Then I decided Belle and Piper were sitting too close to risk it.

Unfortunately.

However, if they got up to go to the restrooms and left Uncle Landry alone on the bleachers, all bets were off. They didn't, much to my displeasure.

The game finally ended, and I stalked over to Belle as West came running over to fucking Uncle Landry.

While West and Piper were occupied with the asshole, I took Belle by the arm and steered her away from everyone.

"Edge -- what are you doing?"

"I need a word," I told her, and had to unclench my jaw.

"What?" she demanded, arms crossed, and her attitude just set me off, as if I was the one in the wrong.

"We were together months," I said. "Months. We were together months before you ever let me meet West and Piper. And now, just one month after you broke up with me, you're bringing another guy around them, letting them call him uncle? Seriously? How well do you even know this guy? Have you checked him out?"

"It's none --"

"For someone who was so reluctant to bring men around her children, it sure didn't take you long to find my replacement. I don't think that's a good move for the sake of the children, and I can't believe you'd do that, Belle."

Her face had started turning red, and at first I thought it was embarrassment at being called out, but then I realized she was mad. Like red-hot mad.

"Are you done?" she demanded, keeping her voice low to avoid a scene.

I tipped my head to the side to indicate I was.

"It's good to know that in addition to thinking I'm just a booty call with baggage, that you think I've suddenly become even more careless than I was with you, and I'm about to begin parading a string of men in front of my children and letting them call them uncle."

Shit. I suddenly had a sinking feeling that I'd made a huge mistake. Again.

"Not that it's any of your business, but that man is my ex-husband's brother, and is, indeed, my children's biological uncle. Landry's a good man and has stayed in West and Piper's lives even though his useless brother decided to abandon them."

Double shit. Oh, yeah, I was fucked.

"Landry and his wife, Phoebe -- who is currently at my house watching their one-year-old -- visit us a couple of times a year. So my children are quite comfortable calling him uncle because he is related to them, and not because I've lost all good sense and am now bringing my booty calls around my children."

"Oh, shit, Belle, I'm sorry," I said, then put my hand on her arm as she began to walk away from me. "I'm sorry. Please, I was jealous thinking you'd moved on --"

She shook her arm out of my hand and shook her head at me. "Save the apologies, Edge. They won't help."

They left the field soon after, and once I'd helped Rob gather the equipment, I got in my car and headed to Belle's.

I needed to get this settled and settled fast. I began knocking on Belle's door, and in less than a minute, she answered the door, a baby on her hip.

And a decidedly unhappy look on her face when she saw it was me.

Chapter 9 (Belle): You Can't Hide

One thing that Edge couldn't be mistaken for was the pizza delivery man. I'd opened the door, expecting our three large pizzas...and there stood Edge, looking at me with the baby on my hip like he'd never seen me before. His face got soft and he smiled.

His smile was beautiful, if I had to be honest.

"Belle, I'm sorry for what I said, what I insinuated earlier," he began. "I didn't stop to think, I just knew I didn't like being replaced, and I definitely have never felt jealous before."

"Edge, you have no right to feel that way even if I wanted to parade a hundred uncles in front of my children."

"But I do feel like it's my right," he insisted. "You all snuck up on me. Belle, I wasn't expecting...my feelings were bigger than I thought, and I didn't know what to do with them.... Shit! It all sounds so lame when I try to justify it, but I'm sorry, Belle. I'm sorry inside like you wouldn't believe because I hurt you and I didn't want to. I'm sorry for hurting you again today with what I said and insinuated, and I mean that like I've never meant anything before in my life."

"He said sorry, Mommy."

Piper. Of course my little ninja girl would sneak up on me when Edge and I were in the middle of a whispered discussion so no one would hear. She had ears like a bat when she heard whispers. My nosy little girl was probably going to grow up to be a spy or a journalist, and she lived to eavesdrop. I'd yet to instill in her how rude it was to listen in to conversations not meant for your ears, but somehow, every time I lectured her on the subject, I felt like I was fighting a losing battle.

And now, she'd heard Edge apologize and mean it, which in our household, was the golden ticket to forgiveness.

"Can he come in and have pizza with us?" she asked, her eyes pleading up at me. Dammit. "Please? He said he was sorry."

Every mother has faced this situation about, oh, a million times. Where we preach forgiveness and repentance to our children...only to not want to extend it to someone else because...because...someone had really hurt our feelings, and we didn't want to forgive him.

"Piper," I began and felt another presence.

"Hey," my brother-in-law said to Edge before turning to me. "We wondered what was keeping you."

"I just --"

"Edge Camden," Edge stuck his hand out. Landry grasped it and introduced himself.

"Edge, huh?" Then Landry slanted a look at me. "This is the baggage handler?"

Eavesdroppers, secret spillers...I needed a vacation. So, this afternoon, while my children had been playing in the yard, Phoebe, Landry and I had been sitting on my lawn chairs, and I may or may not have spilled the beans about the first man I'd been interested in and how he'd broken my heart. Landry had started the conversation by asking who the coach was who had taken me aside for a word at West's game.

After I'd told my story, Landry had looked thoughtful while Phoebe and I grumped about m3n in general and Edge in particular. Then Landry had started in.

"Now, I get it hurt you, Belle. What he said and all," he began thoughtfully. "But I'm a man and I can tell you that we say shit all the time. It's how we're made. We're just popping off and saying stuff without thinking things through and ninety-nine percent of the time we don't even mean what comes out of our mouths."

"I can vouch for that. And even that one percent margin of error he gave himself is iffy," Phoebe said, tossing him a look. Oh, yeah, she knew. "They definitely don't think before opening their mouths. That's just plain fact."

"So, you said this Edge guy apologized, and he kept turning up for two weeks without a word or returned text or call from you? That's dedication to someone he thinks of as just a booty call. If you'd really been that to him, he would have given up after the first day. You said this guy has women chasing after him, so think about it. If he'd really thought of you and the children that way, he would have gladly taken the out. Like, whew! Glad that's over! Instead, he kept coming back, trying to understand why you ghosted him and not liking it at all."

"He's just not used to being the one who ended things. Edge didn't like that I stopped seeing him. Usually, it's the other way around with him. So it was basically male pride."

"Nah. You're still not thinking this through," Landry argued. "If he'd meant what he'd said, no way would he apologize and no way would he become the coach of your son's little league team. He also publicly humiliated this Karen in front of you and set her straight. Would have been the easiest thing in the world to go with her if he'd wanted to get rid of you. In guy speak, he was letting you know he had his eye on you and only on you. If he wasn't interested in you, Belle, he could have gone with easy instead of unimaginably difficult and stubborn and pissed off. When a man's willing to put in that kind of effort to win you back, he's into you."

I crossed my arms over my chest and glared at Landry. Phoebe was kicked back, her baby asleep in her arms, enjoying the show.

"You're wrong. Because he said it and didn't know I was listening. Why say something you don't mean in that case?"

"We just went over this. Because we, as a species, don't think sometimes. We have these horrible things called emotions that we aren't sure what to do with when we really like a girl. It's why we tease you on the playground in elementary school and why our methods don't change all that much when we grow up. We try to deny we're having feelings until we can deny it no longer. This guy, what he's doing...it sounds like he opened his big mouth and his brain wasn't connected. And now he's scrambling. And the fact that he didn't like me around -- that wasn't a dig at you so much as, once again, he was having that big emotion, jealousy, and didn't know how to handle it."

"You know what?" I shot at Landry. "I'm tired of women having to be the only ones who think. I'm a guy isn't a defense. It's your get out of jail free card for bad behavior."

"Preach!" Phoebe added, then cocked her eyebrow at me. "Although, Belle...from everything you've told us, this guy sounds like he's trying to make up for it."

I got up from the chair and fixed them both with a snooty look. "I'm through discussing this and I'm going to hold the baby now."

And I held out my arms to Phoebe and she, with a grin, handed over that bundle of sweetness and innocence.

"You can run, but you can't hide, Belle," she sing-songed to me.

And now, several hours later, standing at the front door with a baby in my arms, Piper at my side, Landry at my back and Edge in front of me, I definitely couldn't run and hide.

"You want to join us for some pizza?" Landry asked him.

"Only if I can pay," Edge negotiated.

With a huge grin, Landry accepted the deal. Without consulting me.

Thus proving that those with the unfortunate xy chromosome combination were never to be trusted.

Chapter 10 (Edge): A Mom Decision

Getting my foot in the door to stop it from figuratively and literally slamming shut on me was a huge step forward. At least, I was taking it that way. My new-found ally Landry -- the man I'd been so jealous of earlier in the day at West's baseball game -- had been an unexpected help when he'd invited me to have pizza with all of them. They could have been serving raw slugs and I would have accepted. I just needed to get myself around Belle more, and this was the perfect way.

Piper couldn't hide how happy she was to see me even though her little face was conflicted and she tugged on her ponytail, her signal that she was uncertain. Belle's face wasn't conflicted in the least. She was pure pissed off.

"Come on, Piper, let's see where Aunt Phoebe is," Landry again proved himself to be friend, not foe.

Piper grabbed her uncle's hand and skipped toward the kitchen with him, and I gently tugged on Belle's arm to stop her from following.

"Belle," I said in low tones so we couldn't be overheard, "I mean it. I'm sorry about what I said and assumed earlier today. I felt horrible about confronting you the way I did, and I know jealousy isn't an excuse, but it's what was driving every word that came spewing out of my mouth."

She laughed, clearly amused. "So I forgive you and then what? Wait to hear more stuff come out of your mouth the next time you're jealous or think I'm not within hearing distance? With your mouth, I want to know how you've made it this far in the Marines without facing a firing squad."

That wasn't the first time I'd heard something like that.

"Belle, give me a chance to make things right with you and the children. Please."

"You're here for dinner, Edge. I didn't invite you, Landry did. So I'll let you stay, but don't mistake that for me welcoming you back into my life. After dinner, if Piper asks you to stay, you'll make your excuses and leave."

"OK," I said. "But I'm going to --"

"What's he doing here?" West asked, coming into the living room from the hallway. His face was angry and if he'd been bigger, I have no doubt he would have tried to throw me out of the house.

"Your uncle invited him to have pizza with us," Belle said neutrally.

"Why?" West protested, his tone conveying that he would have rather eaten with the devil than sit down to a meal with me. "We don't want him here."

"West, you need to mind your manners," Belle said, but I noticed there wasn't a lot of force behind her words like there normally would be if one of the children was being rude.

The doorbell rang and, figuring it was the pizza, I walked to the door, paid the delivery man and came back into the room with three large boxes. Belle had been whispering to West while I was paying for the pizza, and from the look on his face, she'd been chastising him.

"Belle, would you take these into the kitchen so I could have a quick word with West, please? I'd like to speak with him man-to-man."

I saw West straighten up proudly when I said that, and Belle saw it, too. She looked at me for a long moment, then back to West and finally nodded her approval.

"Don't be too long or the pizza will be cold," she warned me. Don't you dare be a jerk to my son.

"Got it," I said, letting her know her message had been received.

"Why'd you wanna talk to me?" West asked once his mother had walked away into the kitchen. I could hear Piper squeal when she saw the pizza boxes.

Because I want you to stop hating me. I want you to want to be around me again. I want you to understand how sorry I am for ever thinking something so awful about you.

That was a little much, so I went with something easier.

"You ever make a mistake, West? Something you said or did that got you in a lot of trouble?"

West's mouth screwed up as he thought.

"I guess so," he said with a shrug. "Yeah."

"How'd you feel after you messed up?" I asked him.

Another shrug. "Not good."

"So you knew you messed up, and it didn't make you feel good, knowing you made a mistake like that."

He thought about my words for a minute. "Yeah."

"Well, that's exactly how I'm feeling right now. I made a really, really bad mistake. I said something mean about your mom and you and Piper, and I've been sorry ever since. If I could take those words back, I would. But I can't, so I'm trying to figure out a way to show you, to show Piper and to show your mom that I'm sorry and I want to be back in your lives."

West looked up at me with those eyes that were a mixture of anger and confusion. It wasn't the look of a little boy; it was the look of an eighty-year-old man who knew a thing or two about life.

"You made my mom cry."

His accusation went straight to the heart of the problem I was facing. I'd hurt Belle, and by extension, West and Piper. Belle was worried about the way I felt about her children, and her son was worried that I'd made his mother cry. If there was a way to feel lower than dirt, I'd like to know because I was face down in it. And rightfully so.

"I did make your mom cry," I admitted to him. "And I've never been so sorry about anything in my life. What I did to her, what I said about her and you and your sister, makes me feel like shit."

The corner of West's mouth twitched at the bad word.

"I want you to know I'm sorry, West. I'm sorry I hurt your feelings, and I'm sorry I hurt your mom and made her cry. A good man doesn't do that. So now, I'm trying to be a better man and I want to show all of you that I want to be part of your family."

Again, this wise little boy thought about my words. "Like our dad? You want to be our dad?"

"That's something down the road that I need to talk about with your mom, West. For now, I want to be back like we were. Where we go out for pizza together, where we watch movies or play board games. I'll keep coaching your team. Things like that."

"I don't know. That's a mom decision."

I kept a straight face. I'd heard that phrase from Belle a million times when Piper and West tried to negotiate for something -- watching a movie that was a little old for them, staying up later, eating something sweet right before dinner.

That's not a decision you two get to make. That's a mom decision.

"It is a mom decision," I agreed with him. "But I wanted you to know what I'm working on. I want to earn your forgiveness and Piper's forgiveness, and I want to be someone your mom can forgive."

"Piper and I just have to say we're sorry and mean it," he said.

Again, I tried not to laugh. Another Belle-ism. Saying you're sorry isn't enough. You have to mean it.

West looked up at me, his expression pure and sincere. "But I think you're going to have to do more than say sorry. To all of us."

He wasn't wrong.

It's scary when a little boy is the smartest one in the room.

Chapter 11 (Belle): Staring Right At Me

- -

Confessional time. Although I may have accused my daughter of being a little eavesdropper, I also may have left out that she comes by it quite honestly.

I can eavesdrop like nobody's business. I not only can, I do.

So, when I told Edge he could speak with West, I snuck through the kitchen, and then went into the back hallway that led to the living room. I stayed out of sight as I listened to Edge explain how he was feeling in terms West could understand. I would have flown from my hiding spot if I thought he was stepping out of line or trying to manipulate my son, but he was explaining things to my boy like he'd always done. Trying to find a similar situation my children had experienced so they could relate it to something else.

The way he was explaining exactly how he'd messed up to West reminded me of a conversation he'd had with Piper not too long after he'd met my children. They'd been quizzing him on what he did for the Marines, and he was trying to explain being an attack helicopter pilot to them and how he had to fly to do his job. She was wondering why he didn't get scared when he had to fly his helicopter and fight the bad guys. Edge had looked at her for a moment, and I could just see him trying to find the right words. One thing I'd always appreciated about Edge was he never gave easy answers to West and Piper to shut them up and stop the endless questions. His answers were always thoughtful and sincere, and he never talked down to them.

"Have you ever danced in a recital before, Piper?"

"Yes."

"Did you just go on stage for the recital and dance your dance for the very first time?"

She'd giggled, like that was the silliest idea she'd ever heard. "No."

"So you practiced your dance before your recital?"

"Lots of times."

"Then when you had to go on stage to dance your dance, maybe you felt a little nervous, maybe a little excited, but you knew you could do it because you'd practiced your dance so many times?"

"Yeah, and I had on my costume."

"Well, I kind of wear a costume, too -- my flight suit and helmet. And I practice and practice and then practice some more, so when I have my recital -- a mission, we call it -- I'm a little nervous, too, but I know what to do because I've practiced so many times."

"You know how to dance your dance," she said to him, nodding.

Edge had looked at her for a minute, then smiled sweetly at her. "Yeah, I know how to dance my dance, Piper."

When Edge and West finished talking, West went into the kitchen.

"You can come out now, Belle."

Damn man.

I came around the corner, but I wasn't looking guilty. "You knew I was there the whole time?"

He shook his head. "No. I heard you whisper that's my boy at the very end when West told me I was going to have to do more than say sorry to all of you."

Edge always did have excellent hearing.

"Listen, I realize it wasn't fair of me to accept the invitation to lunch just because I wanted to be around all of you, so I'm going to take off now, Belle. But that doesn't mean I'm backing off."

My mouth opened before I could think about it. "But you paid for the pizza and people are expecting you to stay."

"Expecting, but not wanting," he said. "And I get it."

"Well, come take some pizza for the road," I pushed. Shut up, Belle. Just let him go. "I'll get you a plate. To go."

OK, there, that was fair. Giving the man who paid for the pizza some slices to go would satisfy my sense of right and wrong.

We walked into the kitchen, and Piper was sitting at the table, West at one end and her aunt and uncle across from her. When she saw Edge, she brightened and patted the seat next to her.

"Come sit next to me, Edge!" She must have intercepted the look West shot her. "What? He said he was sorry, West. And he meant it. I could tell."

Oh, Piper, my sweet, sweet little girl with the big heart.

"That's nice of you, Pipe, but I can't stay, so I'm just going to grab a couple of pieces of pizza and head out."

"You used to stay. Before you said mean things behind Mommy's back. That's what West said you did."

Shit. She might have ninja-like stealth moves to listen in on conversations, but Piper couldn't keep a secret to save her life.

Edge looked sick. Before she became baggage, he'd allowed her to paint his fingernails bright pink and put little bows in his hair. He had seemed to adore her, so I'm sure being called on the carpet by this particular six-year-old killed him.

"Why'd you say mean things, Edge? It's not nice." Her innocent little eyes blinked up at him, honestly wanting an answer to her question.

And then, as he'd always done, he answered her question head on.

"The answer is because I was stupid, Piper. I really was -- and I know that's a bad word, but it's the right word in this case -- and I didn't stop to think before I opened my mouth and said the not-nice things. Because if I had," he stopped and cleared his throat, "if I had stopped to think, I never would have said what I did, and the three of you would still be the most important people in my life."

Blinking a few times to gather himself, Edge said quietly, "I have to run. See you at practice this week."

He was out the door before anyone could say a word to stop him or say good bye. We heard his bike rumble to life and then roar away. And still no one had moved.

West was looking down at his plate, Piper looked sad, and Landry and Phoebe weren't saying a word. We'd all heard the raw pain in Edge's words. It was unmistakable and deep and sincere.

I hadn't considered it before, but hearing what I'd heard in his voice, what we'd all heard, it dawned on me just how badly what he'd said had hurt not just us, but Edge.

Landry and Phoebe and the baby left the day following Edge's visit. When Landry hugged me good bye, he didn't say anything but he gave me a look, and I knew what he was trying to convey. His own brother had walked away from our family without saying anything bad about us. He just didn't want to be part of our family. Edge had said something thoughtlessly mean, but now he was trying to make amends so he could become part of our family.

Edge's pained words stayed with me every day that week, and I found myself thinking about them at odd times.

If I had stopped to think, I never would have said what I did, and the three of you would still be the most important people in my life.

They'd apparently stayed with West, too, because when I was tucking him in one night, he'd looked up at me.

"Do you think Edge feels bad he made you cry?"

"I think he does," I said slowly.

"Are you still mad at him?"

Hmmm. "I'm still not happy with him."

"You liked him."

"We all did," I reminded him.

"Yeah," West said. "Night, Mom. Love you."

Pressing a kiss to his head, I told him I loved him, too.

At practice that week, Edge waved hello to me and smiled his special smile for me the second he saw me. I actually waved back and his smile went to incredibly happy, and then Monica sidled up to me.

"If that man could drop his heart into your pocket to prove how much he cared, he would."

"Not sure about that," I scoffed.

"I've been watching him watch you for weeks. How much experience do you have with men, Belle? Four, five guys?"

"Two," I admitted. "My ex husband and Edge."

"Yeah, well, I have a little more, shall we say. And with all that experience I've had, I've never seen that look in any of my men's eyes. So now, I'm going to hold out for that look. And maybe you might want to think about holding on to that look -- as long as what he did to piss you off wasn't unforgivable."

Now I had not only Edge's words to think about and Landry's look, I also had Monica's words to roll over in my mind. It was exhausting. It was too many words.

At the game on Saturday, I was getting Piper settled beside me on the bleachers when a large crowd of people started shouting and laughing at Coach Edge. I automatically looked over and recognized many of his Marine friends and their significant others from the get togethers at Edge's house. Edge just smiled and shook his head while he focused on the pre-game drills he was running with his little crew.

I glanced over, seeing if any of them had noticed me, and was shocked to see the one face I never wanted to see again.

Karen.

Staring right at me.

Chapter 12 (Edge): Cut Her Loose

As I was running some drills with the boys before Saturday's game, I turned my head when I heard my name being called multiple times.

I saw the guys from my squad and gave them a quick wave before I returned my attention to the boys. The guys had been asking about what I'd been doing on my Thursdays and my Saturdays, so I'd invited them to today's game. Hadn't expected that many of them to show up, but word had spread and I knew the boys would get a kick out of having a larger crowd in the stands for a game. Marines loved any kind of competition and our boys were definitely supported in their efforts during the game.

Every time our team got a hit or made an out, a loud burst of oorah! sounded, and that made the boys burst with pride and spurred them to play even harder. Even West was getting into it, and he grinned almost the whole game. Not surprisingly, with that kind of support and with all the boys playing hard, our team took a healthy lead from the start and kept it until they won the game.

After the two teams and coaches shook hands, the boys had their snacks and drinks and started drifting away toward their families. While some of the parents talked with me, I saw Belle talking with West and Piper and one of the other team moms and her two children, and from the way the children were acting, I could tell there was some begging going on. Maybe a playdate? Would that mean Belle had the afternoon alone and she might be willing to talk with me?

West and Piper gave Belle hugs, and then she waved them off to leave with the other woman and her two children. Belle picked up West's game bag and I walked over to her. My friends -- knowing a bit about my situation with Belle -- were hanging back a little, waiting for me to talk with her, and then I'd talk with them.

"Can I carry that for you, Belle?" I asked as I came up to her, hand out-stretched, but she yanked it out of my reach.

"I don't think your girlfriend would like that so much. Karen's been glaring at me for the entire game, so thanks for that. It was a lot of fun to have to sit through my son's game with her glaring daggers at me from the other side of the bleachers."

Karen was here?

And then, speak of the devil...

"Edge! Belle," an unwelcome voice called.

"Fuck," I muttered. "Belle, I didn't notice her in the bleachers, I didn't know she was here and I sure as hell didn't ask her to be here."

By now, Karen was near us, and those gossipy bitches I served with, scenting a scene -- because many of them also knew Karen and I were no longer friendly -- moved in closer. Fortunately, if there was going to be a scene, everyone else from the team was gone by this point.

"I've been wanting to talk to both of you so we can work this out, like adults," Karen said. "Belle, from day one, you've tried to ruin my relationship with Edge. You're jealous of me and of Edge's and my relationship. You've tried to come between the two of us, and you even sunk so low as to try to use your kids to drive a wedge between Edge and me and make him forget our relationship in your quest for a daddy."

Belle dropped West's bag and took a threatening step toward Karen. "Bitch, I have bats in this bag and if you ever talk about my children or me like that again, I won't hesitate to use them on you."

I quickly stepped in front of Belle, who was bristling and ready to go at Karen hard. But this was my mess and I needed to clean it up.

"There's no relationship between us, Karen. I made that pretty fucking clear in the restaurant that our friendship was over and I wanted nothing more to do with you. Belle never had to try to ruin our friendship because you did that all on your own, by treating Belle like shit behind my back. I haven't had anything to do with you since that day I told you to get gone, and you think I'm fucking playing games? I'm trying my best to win back Belle, and I sure as fuck made it clear to you that Belle was my focus and you and I were no longer friends. I don't even know why the fuck you're here today because I sure as hell didn't invite you or want you here."

That was the first that Karen's confidence seemed to slip. "You're being ridiculous, Edge! I gave you time after that shit you pulled in that restaurant to get over it, to get Belle on board with our friendship -- and there hasn't been one word out of you! Weeks, Edge. You haven't seen me or called or texted me in weeks. So I figured this would be a good place to work things out, and since Belle would be here, I knew the three of us could attempt to talk this out like adults and get past this ridiculous vendetta she has against me."

"Who the hell do you think you are?" I snapped at her, and my voice was loud enough for everyone to hear. "Who the actual fuck do you think you are, to come here and spew this shit? I'm not sure what was hard to understand about my message in the restaurant that day, but I couldn't have made it any plainer that you were out of my life. Gone. Not wanted. For good. No coming back. The choice between you and Belle wasn't even a fucking choice -- it's Belle, hands down, every time."

Before Karen could speak, I leveled my buddies with a glare. "Who the hell told her about the game today? Who was it? Because I know it sure as hell wasn't me."

Miller, one of the newer guys, shook his head. "She's been hanging out with me and asked me about you, and I told her a bunch of us were coming to the game today. She said that sounded like a lot of fun -- and I swear I had no fucking clue you were on the outs with her -- so I said she could ride along with me."

"Well, that's a mistake you won't be making again. If she drove here with you, get her gone now."

"Edge! Seriously? After all we've been through together when your dad died --" Karen tried again, but I'd had enough and was beyond done with her.

"I'm not going to be held hostage to that kind of attempted guilt for something in the past and only a truly shitty person would try to capitalize on someone's grief like that. You blew it with Belle, and it may have taken me a while to get my head out of my ass, but it's out and now you're gone. So let me make this clear in front of everyone for witnesses: I don't want to see you again and I don't want you involved in my life in any way. In short, I don't want one fucking thing to do with you ever again. And, fair warning, if you ever try to come to a game again and glare at Belle or force a confrontation with either one of us, I'll let Belle at you with her bats and provide her with an airtight alibi. Do you need me to repeat any of that or did I put it in terms you could finally understand?"

She'd lost all color in her face and didn't even try to open her mouth. I looked from her to all of my buddies. "Are any of you unclear as to how I feel here?"

They shook their heads, some looking kind of shell shocked. I was known for keeping my cool, so this display of temper wasn't something they were used to seeing.

"Then, Miller, I suggest you get her out of my sight now, and if you're smart or have any sense of self-preservation, cut her loose and find yourself a nice girl."

Miller muttered let's go to Karen, and she hurried after him, head down, not saying a single word.

Chapter 13 (Belle): Helping You Decide?

So, I have to admit a failing of mine.

I freaking loved watching Edge take down Karen. It was petty and vindictive of me, but I enjoyed her humiliation after the nasty shit she'd pulled and the things she'd said about my children and about me. I can be really nice...until you aren't nice to my children. And maybe, depending on my mood, I'll either take the high road or the low road, but my mood was clearly low road all the way today.

Fortunately, my children weren't here to see me hiding an ear-to-ear grin behind the hand covering my mouth. It wouldn't have fooled them as they were used to seeing me clap a hand over my mouth when I was trying to be stern with them but trying to stop myself from laughing at the same time.

"You're smiling, Mommy!" Piper and West would call me out. And they were right. But sometimes...those children of mine popped off with something that I just couldn't help but laugh at, especially when uttered with such innocence.

Anyway, I was hoping that to the Marines gathered around Edge and Karen's standoff, I simply looked like I was covering my mouth in shock. Sort of. If you squinted. And it was dark out. And you were driving by me at fifty miles an hour.

It took everything in me not to do a fist pump or five at certain parts of the takedown. One of my prouder moments? Absolutely not. One of my more satisfying moments? Absolutely, one hundred percent.

When she walked away, head down, with the man who had brought her here, I gave a little wave goodbye. But only in my mind! I didn't actually do it.

As soon as Edge saw Karen take off, he walked over to his fifteen or so buddies to say a few words, shake a few hand and thank them for coming to support the boys. When they began to drift away, Edge walked back over to me, and that's when I realized that I was still standing there like an idiot waiting for him.

"Just so we're perfectly clear," he said, "I was wrong. I should have done that to her the second you and I started dating. I'm sorry I didn't. It was unfair to you and shortsighted of me."

"Yes, you should have. It made me really uncomfortable whenever I was around her and she played queen of the castle at your place and treated me like an interloper."

"That's on me, and I'm sorry that you were uncomfortable because I failed to handle her. There's a lot I regret, Belle. A lot I wish you'd give me the chance to make right."

"Edge, I heard you say I was a booty call with baggage, then two weeks later, you were telling me you were all in. That's a pretty huge turnaround in a short amount of time. What changed? I'm supposed to believe you had a complete change of heart...why?"

"Being without you three," he returned immediately. "I told you, my head may have been slow on the uptake but my heart had it figured out even before you left me. Then those two weeks without you and West and Piper were the longest, most drawn-out weeks of my life. I missed the three of you like you wouldn't believe. I'd walk past that aisle in the grocery store where they sell all that woman stuff, and I'd see a pink bottle of nail polish and think Piper would love that color. Or I'd go past the cookie aisle and think how West would like those Mega-stuf Oreos. And I just thought of you constantly."

He gave me what I called his hear me out face that he used when he was trying to talk me into something.

"I liked the three of you in my house that night, Belle. I liked going in to check on West and Piper and to make sure they were OK. I liked those little faces under my roof. It freaked me out at the time just how much I liked them. I may have said that horrible shit, but I figured out pretty quick that what I'd said to her was just shit. I like my life with you three in it. It's better, it's brighter and it's a helluva lot more fun."

"Edge, do you understand where I'm coming from? Calling my children baggage was horrible. And then you want me to believe it was just a mistake? I'm just supposed to unhear that?"

"No, Belle. Just give me a chance to let you hear some other things, some different things that can help you see I made a horrible mistake. I want to explore this more with you, Belle. I want to get to know the children better. I want to earn back their trust and yours."

She's nothing more than a booty call with baggage.

"Give me the chance to make things right, Belle. I can't stand this distance between us. Before I fucked it all up, did you have feelings for me?"

I didn't want to answer that question. Because we both knew the answer was yes, I did have feelings for him. Still did, to be honest. Very strong feelings that went beyond wanting to strangle him for the booty and the baggage comment.

Edge stepped closer to me. "Belle, if I could re-do any moment in my life, it'd be that moment where I opened my mouth to her. I'd give just about anything to take it back, but since I can't, I'd love to show you going forward that my feelings for you and the children are real and they're strong, and I won't put the four of us at risk ever again."

When my husband and the father of my two children walked away and said, sorry, I don't want any of you, that left a mark, deep and permanent. And I promised myself I'd be careful getting involved with another man, and I'd kept that promise until Edge. Then I'd let him into my life on a very limited basis, waited until I felt we were on a good path, and then I'd allowed him to meet West and Piper.

Once again, the rug had been pulled out from under me.

Third time's the charm? a sweet little voice said in my head.

Fuck that noise, a not-so-sweet voice said.

"I need to think," I told him. "You didn't just hurt me; you hurt West, too, when we overheard you, and then he passed that along to Piper. I need to think, Edge. Think it through thoroughly and make sure my head is clear."

"I get it, Belle. You need to decide."

OK, that was good. That was him understanding my point of view.

And he respected that, spoke to me at practices and games in a friendly way, but he wasn't pushing. In the meantime, I thought about everything he'd said. Ad nauseam.

Two weeks later, I heard the sound of a lawnmower very close to my house. It wasn't my lawnmower, and I knew this because mine was broken and had been for the last two weeks. So, throwing on some sweats and a T-shirt, I ran outside and saw Edge mowing the grass. When he saw me he cut the engine and walked over to me.

"Good morning, beautiful." His greeting was chipper and even out here sweating from pushing the lawnmower, he looked good.

"It's barely seven o'clock and you're mowing the grass? Edge, what are you doing here?"

"Helping you decide?"

Then he grinned at me, and it reminded me so much of West when he was being all happy and eager that I had to clap my hand over my mouth.

Because no way was I going to let him see me smile.

Chapter 14 (Edge): It's Not Your Place

After talking with Belle after the game, I'd agreed to give her time. The weeks dragged for me; the only high point being when I saw her and the children at West's practices and games. Yesterday after practice, he'd told me that their lawnmower was broken. Why had he told me -- very pointedly -- that seemingly random fact?

"How's it going, West?"

Those thin little shoulders moved up and down. "Our lawnmower's broken."

This wise little boy was testing me, I realized. He knew I'd hurt his mother, but he also knew I was sorry. So he'd decided to see if I could become worthy of his mother. It was the only reason I could think of that he'd have told me something like that.

Early the next morning, before I had to head in to work, I'd taken my lawnmower over to Belle's house and mowed the yard. About halfway through, Belle came running out, her surprise at seeing me evident, asking me what I was doing.

"Helping you decide?"

She covered he mouth with her hand, something I knew she did when she was trying not to let the children see her smile at whatever they'd said that struck her as funny.

"Edge, you didn't need to do this. And how did you even know?"

I couldn't stop smiling at this woman. Just being around her for any amount of time was a pleasure after being cut out of her life.

"A little bird told me, Belle. I hate that I made it so you couldn't ask me."

Belle made a little huffing sound. "Piper talks too much."

"It wasn't Piper," I told her but didn't give up my source.

"Well, I don't like feeling obligated to you."

"No obligation," I assured her. "I'm happy to help. But I do need to finish before I head to base, much as I'd love to keep talking with you. You look good, Belle."

"I just rolled out of bed, Edge, and I look it."

I shook my head. "Not to me you don't. See you around."

Then I went back to mowing the grass and I couldn't stop smiling, even during a long, frustrating day at work. That evening, after dinner, I was knocking on Belle's door again, hoping she wouldn't tell me to get lost or slam it in my face.

"Hi, again," I said when she answered the door, West on one side of her. "If you don't mind, I'd like to take a look at your lawnmower, see if I can fix it, get it running for you again."

"Edge, you really don't have to do this." Her protest was automatic, but it wasn't a no.

"I want to help, Belle." I looked down at the little boy standing beside her, eyes watchful. "Maybe West would like to help? I could use the extra hands."

West straightened up at the thought. "Can I, Mom? Then if it breaks again, I could fix it for you."

She held a silent, internal debate, then finally nodded her head. "Sure. I'll go open the garage for you."

West scampered beside me as we walked to the garage and saw the door opening. Belle showed me the lawnmower, described what was wrong and then watched us for a few minutes before going back into the house.

West was a good helper, and he peppered me with questions about everything I did.

What are you doing?

What's that part called?

What does this thing do?

How does an engine work?

Do you think you can figure out what's wrong?

Is it hard to fix?

Do you know how to put this back together?

I answered each question as we worked, explaining in terms he could understand at his age about gas engines. We discovered the problem together -- the spark plug needed to be replaced, as did the filter --and I told him what those two things did. We also cleaned the mower blade very carefully. West ran in to get his mother once we'd diagnosed the problem so he could let her know. Belle and Piper walked into the garage with West.

"Hi, Edge," Piper said shyly. "I just got home. I was over at my friend's." She smiled, showing me she'd now lost both front teeth. She was adorable, her eyes always so bright.

"Hey, Piper," I smiled at her. "Hope you had a good time at your friend's house. Lost another tooth, huh?"

She nodded vigorously and pointed at it, grinning big in case I missed the gap earlier.

Belle listened seriously as West went over the suspected problems, then scrunched her nose a bit. "Is it expensive to fix?"

Shaking my head, I told her the two parts were really cheap. The relief on her face made me want to gather her to me and tell her she didn't need to worry about money, but I knew she wouldn't appreciate it. "I can pick them up on my way home tonight and then come back tomorrow to fix the mower, if that would work for you."

Technically, I had time to do it all tonight, but I wanted to have an excuse to see her and the children again the next day.

"Can I help you fix it?" West asked.

"You can do it all," I promised him. "I'll just tell you what to do."

"I want to help, too!" Piper said.

"You can," I said. "You can help West and me put it all back together."

That made the little princess happy and she grinned at me, delighted.

"I'm going to head out now," I said to them. "See you tomorrow, same time?" I asked Belle.

"Sure," she said. "But let me get you some money for the parts before you go."

I shook her off. "Just pay me tomorrow when I have the receipt."

Which maybe I'd accidentally lose. I wanted to take care of this woman, not have her pay me for parts.

"Thank you," Belle said.

With a smile, I said goodbye to the three of them, and counted the hours until I could see them again. These consequences for my unthinking mouth and stupid actions were killing me.

The next night, I showed up with my tools and the parts in hand. West and Piper were eager to help, so we got started. West, I discovered, took my directions seriously and did everything exactly as I told him to, the tip of his tongue sticking out of the corner of his mouth as he concentrated. He needed very little help, getting stuck just a couple of times where I had to help a bit, and within an hour, he had everything fixed.

"Now I can put it back together?" Piper asked. She'd watched West quietly the whole time he was making the repairs, occasionally telling him good job, West!

"Now you can put it back together," I told her. So I walked Piper through reassembling the mower, and she did a good job, too. If she needed help, I let West assist.

"All done!" she shouted.

"Not yet," I cautioned her. "Once you fix something, you have to test it to make sure it works right. So let's take it out in the yard and start it up."

"And Edge will be starting it up," Belle said from the other side of the garage in her best no-nonsense tone. I hadn't realized she'd been observing, but I wasn't surprised.

"Aw, Mom, can't I do it?"

I raised an eyebrow at West, and he stopped immediately.

The four of us walked to the backyard, and I started the mower and ran it back and forth across the grass several times, Belle and West watching closely and Piper jumping up and down. After a few minutes, I cut the engine.

"It would have stopped way before now," Belle told me. "So I think we can safely say it's fixed."

Piper cheered and West beamed. "A job well done by the young mechanics," I praised them.

"Now, how much do I owe you?' Belle asked.

"Belle, it wasn't much. Don't worry about it."

She gave me the look, and I figured out what to do. "It was about ten dollars," I said.

Running inside, Belle came back a minute later with two fives in her hand. "A word?" I asked her.

We walked off and talked quietly for a minute, and I got her to agree to my plan. We walked back over to Piper and West, and I handed each of them a five.

"You two did really well tonight. You listened and did everything you were supposed to. Thank you for your help."

Their eyes got wide at the money, and they both looked up to Belle, who nodded that they could take it. "You both were good helpers," she said. "What do you say to Edge?"

They both chorused thank you to me.

"See you all at practice," I said.

"Thanks again, Edge," Belle said. And the smile she aimed at me was almost like the ones I used to get from her.

Almost. But that wasn't enough. It wasn't good enough.

At practice that week, when I asked West how he was doing, I found out the hand brake on Belle's bike wasn't working.

"So we can't go on rides together," he said grumpily.

Saturday, after West's game, my helpers and I fixed her bike.

A week later, West informed me that the disposal in the kitchen sink wasn't working, so I replaced it -- and it should have been replaced about five years prior, so I was amazed it'd lasted as long as it had -- along with my eager assistants. That day, Belle followed me out to my car when I was leaving.

"Edge, I'll have another talk with West. You can't keep riding to the rescue."

"Why not, Belle? I want to help you in whatever way I can."

"Because it's not your place."

I walked two steps closer to her. "I want it to be, though. I want you to see that the shit that came spewing out of my mouth is not how I feel. I'm trying to show you that I was wrong and there's nothing I want more than to be with you and the children."

"I'd like to believe that, but I have to think of Piper and West. You didn't just hurt me; West was also hurt and that hurt trickled down to Piper."

I took one final step closer to her.

"Belle, have you asked yourself why West keeps telling me what's broken?"

I could see by the look on her face that it hadn't occurred to her.

Chapter 15 (Belle): No Sense

I was watching Edge carefully, waiting for him to make some misstep again. Honestly, the fastest and easiest way to win over children is with gifts or trips to places they've been begging to go to, but Edge wasn't taking that route. He wasn't trying for shortcuts, and I have to admit, that surprised me.

Instead, he was doing thoughtful things for us, allowing the children to help with his repairs, knowing he could have it done in half the time if he was working alone. But he showed remarkable patience with both Piper and West, answering their endless questions thoroughly and without a hint of irritation.

This is how a father should be.

I absolutely hated that thought every time it popped into my head in the six weeks that followed the lawn mower repair. I stood back as I watched him laugh with the children and then turn more serious and carefully explain and instruct them on the repairs, step by step. He was good with them, extremely patient and kind -- and I had to work hard to remember that he'd called them baggage.

My children seemed to have forgotten that they didn't like him anymore and they basked in his praise. I could tell how much they perked up when he was around, their little faces so intent on their work, and when Edge gave them a good job or that was exactly how it should be done, their little faces broke into wide smiles.

Tonight, they were fixing loose boards on the steps leading to the front porch. Edge had brought some pressure-treated two-by-fours he just happened to have lying around his garage, and he'd stopped by the home center for some stainless steel screws.

"With a self-drilling tip, Mom," West had pointed at the end of the screw, repeating what Edge had just told him.

Piper was currently battling it out with one of the screws, and Edge was right there beside her, tapping the drill every once in a while to make sure it stayed straight. It took effort and concentration on her part with those little hands trying to keep the drill steady, but Piper eventually triumphed.

"You did it, Piper!" West said.

Edge gave her an approving nod. "That wasn't easy, but you stuck with it. Good job."

If he truly thought of my children as baggage, then why had he been coming over several nights a week for the last month to work with them on repairs? Why had he chosen to become a coach for West's team? If you thought that the woman you'd been with was just a booty call with baggage, why go to all the trouble to make amends? He could have easily said good riddance or whew! that was a lucky escape, but he hadn't. He kept coming back at me, apologizing and trying to make amends.

Given his looks and profession, I was under no illusions that Edge couldn't easily and quickly find a replacement for me. He had his choice of women -- women who didn't have baggage, who were free to do whatever they wanted whenever they wanted without having to take two little lives into consideration.

Trying to reconcile his thoughtless words with his thoughtful actions gave me a headache because it didn't make sense. I couldn't reconcile the two. How did thirty seconds of nasty words compare to weeks and weeks of his time and energy? Who was the real Edge? Which of the men I'd encountered was he? His apologies to me for what he'd said had seemed sincere.

If I had stopped to think, I never would have said what I did, and the three of you would still be the most important people in my life.

I often thought of West's question to me after the pizza night debacle.

Do you think Edge feels bad he made you cry?

I was pretty positive he did, now more than ever. He was giving my children the most precious gifts you could give to anyone: Time and attention. Kindness. Patience. Genuine praise. He was giving me time to decide, too. He never pushed to stay after whatever repair project was finished, never asked for more than being able to help us. He didn't push me to go out with him, never tried any underhanded tricks with the children to get us all out together, like asking if they wanted to go out to eat or something like that.

Monica's conversation at the ballfield the one day had also stayed with me.

"If that man could drop his heart into your pocket to prove how much he cared, he would."

"Not sure about that."

"I've been watching him watch you for weeks. How much experience do you have with men, Belle? Four, five guys?"

"Two. My ex husband and Edge."

"Yeah, well, I have a little more, shall we say. And with all that experience I've had, I've never seen that look in any of my men's eyes."

He might not be pushing, but Edge couldn't hide the look in his eyes when he saw me. It was affectionate, it was sweet, it was caring, but it was also desire and heat.

"Mom," West was calling for my attention, which had clearly wandered. "Come step on the new boards! Come walk down the steps. They don't move anymore!"

Smiling at the pride in my son's voice, I stepped off the porch and walked down the steps, then turned back to the three of them and smiled. Maybe it was time to reach back out, test the waters a bit.

"You've all done a great job, and since tomorrow's not a school day, what do you say we go out and get some ice cream to celebrate?"

My two jumped up and down shouting yes, obviously. Edge looked at me, hesitant, not sure if he was included in the invitation or not.

"You two run in and wash your hands," I told Piper and West. "Then we can get going."

They ran off, but at the door, West turned back to Edge. "You coming, too?"

"Let me talk with your mom before I give you an answer," Edge said, not willing to commit because he didn't want to overstep.

West accepted that and followed Piper into the house.

"I didn't mean to put you on the spot," I apologized. "I didn't think that maybe you might have something else going on tonight."

"I'd love to go, Belle," he said, stepping closer to me, "But I wasn't sure if you meant for me to come along, too, and I didn't want to assume."

"You were definitely included in that offer," I said. "You've been doing a lot of work around here since my son is apparently set on dragging you into the home repair business, and I thought you could all use a little reward tonight for your efforts."

"I know I still have a lot to prove," he said, "so don't worry that I'll think this is the all-clear for me. It's ice cream with the three of you, no more, but I'll be honest and tell you that I've never been so happy to be going out for dessert."

"Well, who wouldn't be excited for some ice cream?" I teased him gently to lighten the mood.

Before he could say anything, Piper came out the door, yelling, "Let's go! Let's go!"

West followed right behind her, but quietly.

"Did you decide?" West asked Edge.

"I did," Edge said. "And I'd like to go, if that's OK with you."

"Yep," West said without hesitation, then asked if we could go in Edge's truck, which had a crew cab.

"West, we'll have to go in my car because I have the booster seats," I reminded my son.

The booster seat was a huge point of contention with West because I followed the guidelines religiously and at only four feet seven inches, he was still under the recommended guidelines for no longer needing a booster.

"I have booster seats in the truck," Edge said unexpectedly.

All three of us turned to look at him. "Why?" West asked.

"I got 'em a while ago," Edge said nonchalantly. "Just in case."

I wanted to ask, but wouldn't, so I was delighted when West dove right in. "In case what?"

Edge turned a little pink. "In case your mom ever needed me to take you somewhere. In case she ever had car trouble and was out with you and I came to pick you up. So we can go in the truck if it's OK with your mom."

I nodded, and they ran off. I heard Piper yell, "Mine's pink!" and they disappeared into the truck's backseat.

"How long have you had them?" I asked, no longer able to contain my curiosity. A couple weeks? A month?

He turned even pinker but wouldn't look away from me. "I got 'em the same day they slept at my house. Ready to go?" Then he hurried off to open my door.

I stood still for a minute, thinking this through. He'd bought the seats the same day that he'd later referred to me as a booty call with baggage? That made no sense.

"Belle?" Edge prompted me after I hadn't moved from my spot.

Giving my head a shake, I walked over and got into the passenger seat, and then he closed my door. Deciding to think about the seats later, I just enjoyed the evening, the children's happy chatter and the side looks Edge kept shooting at me.

He kept sending me those looks as we ordered our ice cream, and snagged a table outside to enjoy both the beautiful night and the ice cream. After we finished and little mouths and hands were wiped clean, Edge took us home, walked us to the door and said good night.

Then after I put the children to bed, I got out my phone and sent Edge a text.

Chapter 16 (Edge): My Intentions

By any chance, do you have some time tomorrow to help me fix something?

I looked at the late-night text from Belle. This was new. It'd always been West mentioning things around their house that needed fixing and Belle protesting at first and then allowing me to help. Now, she was the one actually doing the asking, and I hoped it was more of a rhetorical question; I hoped that I'd been showing Belle these last weeks that I'd do anything for her and the children.

Of course. What time? And what needs fixing so I can bring the right tools?

The three little dots rippled for a minute.

No tools required. Come around six and have dinner with us.

The dots rippled at me again.

If you want and don't have other plans.

This woman. She was the only plan I had, and even if I'd had something scheduled, I would have canceled it without a second thought.

No other plans. Except to win you and the children back. But I didn't think that needed saying in a text.

I'd love to come to dinner. Can I bring anything? Dessert?

She took a second to respond. No, thank you. I have it covered.

Then I'll see you tomorrow around six. Good night, Belle.

Good night, Edge.

Belle had invited me to dinner and asked for my help herself, which made me feel like a fucking teenage boy the night before his first date with the girl of his dreams. I was hoping her texts to me meant I was making progress. That she was beginning to see how I was trying to make things right. That she could count on me.

That night, I went to bed with the biggest damn smile on my face. And it stayed on my face the next day at work, while I checked the time at least once every ten minutes. Six o'clock couldn't get here soon enough.

At exactly six, I was knocking on Belle's front door. She answered it, with West and Piper at her side. They were all smiling at me, and I was smiling right back. I held out the bright purple, pink and blue bouquet of flowers to Belle.

"These are for you, Belle. Thanks for asking me to dinner."

"Thank you," she said, her smile turning shy. "They're beautiful."

Not even close to you, sweetheart.

Then I held out a little pink bakery box to Piper. "These are for you, Piper. Some sugar cookies."

Her smile got bigger since those were her favorite cookies lately because they have pretty icing, Edge, and she hugged my waist and said thank you.

I handed the other pink box to West. "And these are chocolate chip cookies for you. They only had pink boxes at the bakery, buddy. Sorry about that."

He grinned up at me. "I don't care. Thanks, Edge!"

"Boxes in the kitchen on the counter, please, you two."

The children ran off to do as Belle requested. "Come on in," she said, stepping back so I could come in. "I haven't mentioned to them that I asked you to help fix something. It's kind of...a surprise for them, in a way, so are you OK with not saying anything about it to them?"

"No problem, Belle."

"Dinner's almost ready," she said, again with that bit of shyness that made me curious. "Let me put these in some water and then it won't take long to get everything ready and on the table. I made beef stew, salad and some fresh bread."

That was my favorite meal, and Belle knew it. I was hoping that was another good sign because I missed this woman and her children. The past months without them only solidified in my mind that I wanted back in their lives and to be more to all of them.

Fifteen minutes later, the four of us were seated around the table, Belle's hearty stew and bread practically making my mouth water.

But not as much as the woman sitting across from me.

Piper talked about her ballet recital the next month, West wanted to talk about strategies for the game coming up (it was a team they'd lost to before in the season), and Belle and I managed to smile at each other often throughout their rapid-fire conversation.

Through it all, I felt like a family man, and instead of that concerning me, I found that it settled something in me. It felt comfortable, not scary in any way, just right, as if I were back where I belonged.

After dinner was cleaned up, with Belle putting food away, West and Piper clearing the table and me rinsing the dishes and putting them in the dishwasher (with the occasional no, this goes here from Belle), we played some board games until Belle said it was time for the children to get ready for bed.

"Do you mind waiting a minute while I oversee the bedtime routine?"

Belle, the way I'm feeling, I'll wait a long time.

"Take your time," I told her.

She hurried off, and a few minutes later, Piper came out, freshly-washed face, freshly brushed teeth and a purple nightgown on. I stood up.

"All ready for bed, Piper?"

"Yes! Mommy said I could come say good night. And thank you for the cookies," she said.

"You're welcome, Piper."

Then she threw her arms around my waist and hugged me, and I hugged her back.

"Good night, Pipe," I said, and saw Belle was standing by the hallway, smiling.

"Come on, honey," Belle said. "Time for bed."

West came in as Belle and Piper left for Piper's bedroom.

"Thanks again for the cookies, Edge," he said. "I'm glad you came to dinner."

"Me, too, and you're welcome for the cookies."

"G'night."

"Good night, West."

Then West turned back to me. "You're not bad. You just said something bad. That's what Mom always says."

Fuck if that didn't hit me right in the heart.

"I did, and I hope you know how sorry I am for what I said, West."

He nodded at me, then went to bed.

About ten minutes later, Belle came out and I stood up from the couch. "They're both out," she announced softly.

Once she sat down on the couch, I did, too. "So, what's the secret project you don't want Piper and West to know about?"

Her cheeks turned pink. "It's not, really. A secret project, I mean."

"You said you wanted help fixing something that was kind of for them?"

She blushed harder. "What I wanted help fixing, Edge, was our relationship. If it ever was really one. I think it was, but I don't want to overstep, but you said you wanted to win me back, but if you've changed your mind, I get it, but it doesn't seem like you have --"

She wanted help fixing our relationship. That was all I heard at first before I realized she was talking a mile a minute without pausing to take a breath in her embarrassment. And embarrassed was the last thing I wanted Belle to feel.

I picked up her hand, which was ice cold from nerves. "Slow down, Belle. I'm in. I want to fix us, too."

"Really?" She sounded relieved and hopeful.

"Really," I assured her.

"I mean, it seemed like it because you were over here all the time fixing things, but then I thought it might be guilt even though you said it wasn't and --"

"Belle," I said, wanting her to slow down. "Belle, I've been trying to show you that I want to give us a try. We didn't get that far before I blew us all to hell, but I want to see where we can take this. Not dancing around it this time, not leaving anything unspoken and playing it by ear, but actually talking it out and saying what we are."

"And what if I'm uncomfortable with something this time?"

"This time I listen. This time I don't play it off. We talk about it."

"That would be good."

"And, Belle, I can't believe this is going to come out of my mouth, but I think we started backwards, with what we both thought was going to be a one-off and that's all it was going to be, and it kind of snowballed from there, but this time I'm good with taking it slower. So we can focus on the right things, keeping West and Piper in mind. I don't ever want to hurt any of you again."

"I still don't understand the two parts of that day," she said quietly. "You bought my children booster seats for your truck the same day you said I was a booty call with baggage. That doesn't make any sense to me."

"I think two parts of me were battling it out, Belle. Mind versus heart. The stupid part, my mind, won out that night, but deep down where I wasn't ready to admit it, you three were more to me. I was making a decision without having to admit to anything with the booster seats, and then I pushed back hard against myself when Karen was running her mouth about wedding bells and me being an insta-daddy. And at the time, I even thought I meant it. Then you took yourself and the children out of my life, and I swear my life went to shit. You ghosted me, and I couldn't get you to talk to me for two of the worst weeks of my life."

"You deserved it."

"One hundred percent. I lost you, I lost West and I lost Piper just as we'd started to become something, even if I didn't know what that something was, exactly. And even worse, I hurt you three, and that ate at me constantly."

I tried to come up with something that could convey to her a little of what I'd felt.

"I don't know how to describe it, Belle, other than that feeling you get when you lose your wallet. And I know that's a crazy comparison, but it's that sickening feeling that you get when you realize you've lost something that important to you. All you can think about and focus on is finding it again. You want it back, you need it back and you won't stop until you find it again. Whatever it takes to get it back, you'll do it. And the whole time, you're kicking yourself because you were careless with something that's critical to you, and the thought that it might be lost to you forever is a real punch to the gut."

Belle's lips quirked. "I've never been compared to a wallet before."

"Losing you shook me loose from my complacency, Belle. It was an alarm that jolted me awake. So I don't want to be complacent this time. I want to be clear in my intentions."

"And what are your intentions?"

"We're going to take it slow, but I intend to win your heart, Belle."

Chapter 17 (Belle): Back Here With Us

When a man like Edge tells you his intentions, he means business. When he finally sorts his shit and figures things out, when he tells you he's coming after you and intends to win your heart, your life is about to change.

My mind conjured a visual, like a scene from a movie, where I was standing at the edge of a cliff and an attack helicopter came rising up slowly, its sights set on me, and Edge was piloting the gunship. Of course, considering his career, who else would be flying the helicopter? Then he pulled the trigger and hearts and cupids came out of the barrels of the guns, right before he blew me a kiss.

When he'd declared he was going to win my heart, I'd given him a speculative look. "My heart comes with two littler hearts, Edge. Two hearts that are actually more important than mine when it comes down to it. If it was just my heart at stake, I'd say win away, but you have three hearts to win."

With a smile, he'd moved closer to me on the couch, his hands going to my thighs. "I know, Belle. I'm very aware it's more than you and all that it means. That's why I want us to take it slower this time, to build things from the ground up intentionally. I'd like to think the last few weeks have been pointing toward that."

I thought of him coaching West's team, of all the repairs he made to things around the house, even the booster seats he'd bought and installed in his truck for the children. Of the way he kept persisting.

"They have. You've been repairing the damage. With all of us, and not only that, you've been doing it the right way, with your time and patience."

"Got plenty of patience, Belle, but time may be trickier when I get deployed in five months."

He'd mentioned a long time ago that he got deployed for about six months every year-and-a-half to two years. I think he'd been stateside for the last eighteen months, so he was due.

"You going to be OK with that?" he asked. "It's not easy on relationships."

"I think I would be, but like anything between us, we won't know until we try. I knew going into this who you were and what you did for a living. I know we started completely casually, but if I wasn't OK with this, I wouldn't have let you meet the children."

He pressed a kiss to my lips, a kiss that made me want to say, screw slow. Let's go!

"All we can do is try, Belle. That's all I'm asking."

"I'm definitely willing to try, Edge."

He began by asking me out on dates. Not dinners that we knew would end in sex, but real dates where we talked even more than we ever had, and there were no expectations at the end of the night except a good kiss. A really good kiss. The kind of hot, wet kiss that left you panting for more, feeling needy and wet and...shit. This going slow plan sucked. But every time I thought that, I remembered Piper and West, and how things had once gone sideways with this man and how their little hearts had been bruised because I hadn't been vigilant enough.

I still berated myself for that, and I determined to go slow with Edge if it killed me. With the way I felt when he tore himself away from me to head home after our dates, I was afraid it might.

"This is killing me, too, you know," he said one night after he'd walked me inside and the sitter had left. Edge had me pressed up against the front door, every inch of us pressed together, his hard to my soft, and his mouth was tormenting mine, pulling away every time the kiss got deep, then coming back for an even deeper kiss. Attack and pull away on an endless, teasing loop.

He'd put his forehead against mine and told me, "You tend to forget this anticipation, this build up, how much fun making out is, where you're going at it until you think you're going to explode. It's like the longest edging in my life," he said, his voice thick with desire and frustration. "I kind of like it."

"Just not too much," I warned him before he started it again. I felt him smile against my lips, and I thought of how much I liked that, how much I liked this man.

Maybe more than liked him, but I was a coward and was waiting for him to say it first.

In addition to dating me, he also planned outings for us with the children, too.

"I want to take the lead on this," he'd said. "I'll plan things, run the ideas past you and then I'll make them happen if you approve."

And he had. At first, when he'd said he wanted to make plans, I was afraid they'd be over-the-top outings sure to win the children's hearts in case there was any lingering reticence. But I should have known better. He planned simple and sweet things that sometimes didn't cost anything but made the most impact and gave us wonderful memories. He went all out, and the accumulation of little gestures spoke to me, to West and to Piper.

After three months of Edge's Win Their Hearts initiative, when I went into West's room one night after putting Piper to bed, my little boy was sitting criss-cross applesauce on his bed, a serious look on his face.

"What're you thinking about, buddy?" I asked, sitting beside him.

"Edge," he said in that straightforward way of his. So West. Ask him a question and he'd tell you the answer, no hedging.

"What about him?"

"I like him again." He looked up at me. "Is that OK, that I'm not mad at him anymore?"

"Oh, West, honey. Yes, of course."

"I figured," he said solemnly, "since he said sorry. But I wanted to check."

Kissing the top of his head, I put my arm around him and hugged him close to my side.

"Do you like him again, too, Mom?"

"I do. Very much."

And the slight strain on that little face eased, and West, my sensitive little boy, went to bed lighter in spirit. When I repeated the conversation to Edge that night, he got quiet.

"I hate that I fucked up the way I did," he said.

"We all make mistakes," I reminded him. "Why should you be perfect?"

"I get mistakes, Belle. But mine not only hurt you but our children."

I froze, wondering if he realized what he'd said. Since he didn't say any-thing, I just responded lightly, "It'd be one thing if you hadn't fixed it, but you did."

A week later, Edge called me, his voice tense. "Belle, I was just asked to fill a deployment spot for one of the pilots who just broke his arm and his leg."

"Oh, no," I said. "Is he going to be OK?"

"Yeah, Merle's going to be fine. He's lucky the car accident wasn't worse than it was, considering he was T-boned, but he was supposed to leave in two weeks. So they asked me to go in his place."

"Oh, well, it's a couple of months ahead of schedule, but this just means you get back sooner, right?"

He laughed, relieved. "Yeah. Let's look at it that way," he said, amusement lacing his tone. "I love your attitude, Belle. It helps more than you know."

Edge and I discussed it some more and decided to tell the children at dinner to give them some time to think about it and ask any questions.

"So, you're leaving us?" West asked.

"With my job, I have to go away sometimes," Edge explained. "I'll be away for six months flying my helicopter. You want to go get the bag by the front door that I brought in, please?"

West was off like a shot and came back with the bag. "So I got you both calendars and some markers, and I thought we could work on them tonight so you know when I'm leaving and when I can come back to you. We'll put some dates on there, like a countdown, and every day you can cross off another square and I'll be one day closer to coming back to you."

"I have sparkly pens!" Piper crowed.

Once the kitchen table was cleared, we marked the day Edge would leave, the day he'd come back and added things like, "Five months left!" and "Three months to go!" and other encouraging milestones.

"That's a lot of days," West said as he flipped through the pages.

"It is," Edge said. "But we can hope it goes fast. And I'll write you letters and we can do video calls as often as we can and maybe you could write me letters, too."

"And send goody boxes," I promised after Piper and West agreed to write. "We'll research that, what the best things are to send, so we'll know what to do for Edge."

The next two weeks flew by and Edge made sure to see us as much as he could. "Listen," he told me one night. "I have to get on that plane early tomorrow, and I don't want you to come send me off."

"But --"

"No, listen, Belle. Please. I want to help put Piper and West to bed tonight, give them hugs and kisses and say we're starting the countdown. Then I want to come here and spend the night with you, Belle, just hold you all night, and in the morning, I want to give you a kiss so you'll think about me while I'm gone. Then I want to slip away while you're all still in bed so I can have that in my head while I'm away, not you with all the other families, crying and saying goodbye. That's always depressed the hell out of me."

"Whatever you need, Edge." I was determined to be supportive and give Edge whatever he needed.

"But when I come back, Belle, when I come back, I want you and Piper and West waiting with all the other families, and I want to see your smiling faces first thing."

I cleared my throat and told him something I'd found online when I was looking up things to say to a loved one who was deploying.

"We'll be there, I promise. And while you're over there, you concentrate on taking care of business and being safe, and I'll take care of everything back here."

Edge's eyes were shining. "I love you so much, Belle."

I gulped down the tears that were threatening. That was the first time he'd told me he loved me.

"I love you, too, Edge."

The next morning, the children were still sleeping when Edge sat on the side of the bed next to me.

"I'll call when I can, Belle." He pulled out his phone and aimed the camera at me. "Let me take a video of you while you look so sleepy and well-loved. Could you say something to me so I can watch this while we're apart?"

My smile was soft. "Edge, I love you so much. Be safe and I'll be waiting right here for you, loving you and missing you and counting down the days until you're back here with us."

The children looked forward every night to crossing a square off their calendars. They drew pictures and wrote letters to Edge; we researched what to send soldiers who were deployed. Every week we sent him packages, and we were excited when he was able to call us and we could see his face.

Every call ended with Edge looking intently into the camera. "I love you all. I miss my family."

When he came home, we were all there with our smiling faces, as requested.

And Edge was there with a diamond ring.

Epilogue (Edge): To Be Cherished

I'd been deployed multiple times before, but I'd never felt each day drag so slowly. I'd actually made my own calendar pages so I could cross the days off and show Piper and West whenever we FaceTimed so they'd know I was counting the days until I could return home, too.

There was so much to get back for. I had my Belle, West and Piper. I could picture their faces so clearly in front of me, and I wondered what they were doing all the time. How they were doing. If they were missing me as much as I missed them. After the first two hundred times I watched Belle's video telling me she loved me, I lost track of how often I hit that play button, but if it'd been a Tik-Tok video, I would have made it viral on my own.

Almost as often, I patted the engagement ring for Belle that I carried with me everywhere, like a talisman in my pocket. I'd bought it before I knew I was going to be filling in for Merle on his deployment, so I'd taken it with me to remind me of everything I had to look forward to when I returned home.

When I woke up, I patted my pocket. When I began work for the day, I patted my pocket. When I was getting ready for a flight, I patted my pocket. And when I was falling to sleep every night, I patted my pocket. That ring went everywhere I did, and I had big plans for how I was going to propose to Belle. It was going to be just the two of us in an intimate, romantic setting, complete with candles, rose petals and soft music, and I'd tell her about how much I loved her then I'd ask her to marry me. We'd have champagne on hand to toast our engagement, then we'd go home and tell the children...

But, the best laid plans of mice and men and all that shit because the second I returned home, the very second I saw my little family waiting for me with so many other families, all my plans went out the window. I fucking ran to them, hugged them all...then dropped to my knee right in front of Belle, pulled out the ring and asked her to please be my wife. Not even a candle or rose petal in sight.

Fortunately, she said yes and began crying so hard I had to pull her into my chest and hold her while Piper and West pressed close, and all around us, the other families were cheering and crying for us.

A few months later, West walked his mom down the aisle, then came to stand by my side, while Piper was by her mom's side. They stayed right there because Belle and I wanted them to have the best seats in the house while Belle and I recited our vows and made our promises to each other. After I was told to kiss my bride, Belle took my arm, holding her flowers, her free hand holding Piper's and my free hand holding West's. It was our first official walk as a family.

Then, a couple of months later during dinner, we were talking, and I brought up a subject to West and Piper that Belle and I had been talking about for a while.

"I want you two to think about something," I said seriously. "I'd like to adopt you both, so you'd have my last name and I'd officially be your dad."

"You're not our dad now?" Piper asked, eyes wide.

They'd both started calling me Dad right after Belle and I returned from our honeymoon. West and Piper had brought it up at dinner, the same day we'd picked them up from Landry and Phoebe's house. Their aunt and uncle had taken care of them while we were on our honeymoon. When we sat down to dinner that night, West brought it up and Piper provided support. It seemed a lot of important issues were discussed around the dinner table when you had a family, and that night I'd been humbled they both wanted to call me Dad.

"I am your dad," I hurried to reassure her before those sparkly eyes lost their sparkle. "But there are papers we would sign to make it legal and we could change your last names to mine if you want."

"West Camden," West said, trying it out loud.

"Pi-peeeeeerrrr Caaaaaaam-dennn," his sister added, announcing it like she was a football player taking the field.

"OK," West said to me after he finished cracking up at his sister. "I want you to adopt us."

"Me, too," Piper said.

"You don't have to answer right now," I tried again.

"You have your answer," Belle said to me firmly and gave me a look that, even as a newly-married man, I already recognized. Cease and desist; we'll discuss it later.

Belle smiled at me later that night after we'd put the children to bed, and I was leaning over my wife in our bed.

"Did they decide too fast?" I asked her.

"There's not too much to consider besides how cool the new last name sounds at this age, Edge. To them, the day you married me, you became their father. They don't have a concept about the legalities or what those mean or the rights you'll have now. To Piper and West, it's the name change. That's it. That's what adoption means to them."

A few months later in early summer, we appeared in family court to make the adoption official and legal. While we were waiting our turn to be called up front, I leaned over to Belle and pointed to the little family in front of the judge right then. The little girl, dressed in a yellow sundress with daisies on it and her hair up in two pigtails, was held tightly in her daddy's arms. Her baby sister, dressed the same, was held in her mother's arms.

"I wouldn't mind a couple more," I whispered.

"That can be arranged," Belle whispered back. We'd been talking about adding to our family for the last few months, and I liked to remind Belle every once in a while, and she did the same.

I smiled at her, kissed those lush lips of hers and then looked at our two children. West was serious looking in his little blue suit that matched mine, right down to the pale green ties Belle had purchased for us.

"Green symbolizes new beginnings," she told each of us. "So we're all wearing green in one way or another for our big family day."

Piper was wearing a sweet white dress with green flowers scattered over it, and Belle was wearing a not-so-sweet but incredibly smoking hot green and white dress.

My family. My family. I kept sneaking glances at all of them as we waited to appear in front of the judge and my mind went back to the time I had jeopardized what I had. I thought of what could have happened had Belle and the children not forgiven me, and my insides iced over at the thought that another man could have swept in and taken my family as his own.

Be careful with your words.

The officiant who married us knew nothing of the horrible shit that had come spewing out of my mouth that Belle and West had overheard, almost ending us forever, but his words of advice to us during the short homily had struck me hard.

Be careful with your words.

Guard each other's hearts.

Protect your love with diligence.

Even without his sound advice, I'd already learned that lesson in such a way I'd never make that mistake again. I had to guard Belle's heart as well as Piper's and West's and the hearts of any other children we had. Every decision had to be weighed and discussed with Belle before making it. It's the easiest thing in the world to have a family but the most difficult to care for it properly at all times and never take it for granted.

When Belle's beautiful eyes looked at me, when West's earnest eyes looked up to me, when Piper's eyes twinkled happily at me, I realized how much was depending on me to get it right. There was nothing I wanted more.

Belle and I began trying in earnest for another child a few months after the adoption was complete, just to give ourselves a little bit of breathing space. Piper, for the first few months after appearing before the family court judge, continued to call out her new name randomly and then it settled down and was no longer new. When she grew up, she told me that she never remembered not being a Camden. West strutted around in his new baseball jersey with Camden emblazoned across the back that first season after the adoption.

"Just like yours, Dad," he said, since I was continuing as an assistant coach in the new season and I had Camden across the back of my jersey.

"Just like mine," I said, and I wasn't sure if Belle's hormones from her pregnancy were contagious, but I choked up. Belle looked at me and laughed sympathetically because she was teary eyed, too.

I'd been asked to become a helicopter pilot instructor, and Belle and I discussed it and I accepted the assignment. It would mean no more deployments and more stability for our family. That turned out to be a good thing with our baby boy on the way.

West was excited at the thought of a little brother and Piper was thrilled she was going to get her own personal baby doll.

A year after Jackson was born, Belle got pregnant again and nine months later our daughter River was born. With her birth, we knew our family was complete.

I looked at my children and thought I'd just about kill anyone who looked at them and saw them as baggage. As burdens.

"I was a fucking asshole, Belle," I said to her one night when we were wrapped around each other.

And just like always, my wife knew what I was talking about. "Yeah, you were," she agreed. "But you un-assholed yourself and made it up to us. Beautifully, I might add. It helped that I loved you."

"Thank God for that because I couldn't lose you, Belle. I knew that." I kissed her. "If you hadn't taken me back, I wouldn't have four beautiful children. And I wouldn't have a wife I loved more than anything."

Be careful with your words.

Guard each other's hearts.

Protect your love with diligence.

Now that I knew what I stood to lose, the love that was at risk, I made sure I lived that advice every day. The love I gave to my family, well, they gave it right back to me, and we all understood what it was to be cherished.

It was the best feeling in the world.